**Please return this book on or before the due date below**

12/08/16
19/08/16
26/08/16

SK

# AS HEAVEN DOES

## GABRIEL
## WILLIAMSON

Published in the United States by Cerulean Sky Press, an imprint of DP & Sons Publishers, Portland, Oregon USA. Published in the United Kingdom by CJH, Ltd.
www.ceruleanskypress.com

Library of Congress Cataloging-in-Publication Data
Williamson, Gabriel Sean, 1998—
As Heaven Does / Gabriel Williamson.—1st ed.
p.  cm.
1. Angels and angelic lore—Fiction.    2. Heaven—Life in—
Fiction.   3. Angels—Homosexual attraction between—Fiction.
4. English life—Contemporary—Fiction

ISBN-13:  978-1530897315      ISBN-10:  1530897319

Printed in the United States of America or the United Kingdom

*Book Designed by Wilson Rushbrook*

First Trade Paperback Edition

For Erica

# PROLOGUE

My name is Aidan. I'm 17 years old. I live in a little village on the coast, called Orvale. It's a quiet sort of place, and not much happens here. The local people are friendly, and everyone knows everyone else. We have many conflicting personalities, but somehow we all just gel together as one town; it's very peaceful. Even I, who only came to the town relatively recently, feel as if I've lived here for my entire life.

See, I only arrived here last year. Well, I say arrived. I washed up on the beach and was found by someone who would later become my best friend, but I woke up with no memories. I'd got amnesia, and even now I can't remember what my life was like beforehand. But nobody in town knew me, so evidently I wasn't from here.

In addition to this, I have dreams. Not dreams, as in aspirations, we all have them, but nightmares. Horrible nightmares, where all I can process is a stormy night, and a silhouette standing in front of me, assaulting me. I've had them since I woke up on the beach that first morning, and they've become part of who I am. It was particularly bad during a school residential trip. *There's the kid who has night terrors,* they said. *He's frightened of his pillow.* Heh. If they only knew…

Anyway, enough of my murky past. I live in the present. Our past doesn't define us by who we were previously. Nor can the future be ascertained to show who we will become. It is the here and now that dictates who and what we are as individuals. Or at least that's what I believe.

Right now I'm just sat on my back porch, looking out over the bay. My house is fortunate enough to give me a great view of the beach and the sea. It's also fortunate that my boss is so lenient with me as to pay me enough to keep the house up. I work at a restaurant in town, and even though I'm not legally an adult my boss made the decision to pay me just over the minimum wage for a legal adult, due to my circumstances being a student with no known relatives. Plus it's mainly because my boss is such a kind man. The rent is cheap here, and I've acquired the skills to cook for myself from the restaurant's chef who, may I say, makes great pulled pork!

So my colleagues at work have really taken me in,

essentially, and they're like the family I never knew. I plan on going to university next year, and one of my colleagues could be going with me to the same place, so it's not as if I'm alone. I hope to study Performance, as I adore the stage and singing, and my colleague is a brilliant singer so we're probably going to end up on the same course; she's hoping to become an actress.

So as I was saying, I'm looking out over the sea. I glance across to the bay and watch the boats swaying in the wind, rolling over the waves that lap at the sand. A knock sounds at my door; I turn, walking straight through the living room and kitchen to the front of the house.

"Hey Ben." I smile as my best friend appears in the doorway.

"Hey man, you working tomorrow?" He's a frequent visitor to the café, and I think it's because he secretly likes the waitress I work with.

"Yep, but I'm on the evening shift tomorrow night, so if you want to see me you'll have to come beforehand, I start at half five."

"Okay, is Cynthia working tomorrow?"

"Yeah but she gets off when I start, she's on the lunch shift eleven 'til half five, sorry dude."

His face visibly falls, and I laugh. "What?"

"You look like you've just kicked a puppy; is the only reason you even come to the restaurant to see her?"

He gets slightly defensive. "Course not, I come to see you!"

"I work in the kitchen. You can't see me when I'm working. You know that."

"Damnit…"

I smirk. "So do you want to come through, or are you just gonna stand out here looking like a lemon?" I lead him out to the back of the house, grabbing a bottle of cola and two glasses as I do so. "Drink?"

"Thanks, I need the sugar, I have a test tomorrow and my revision is glaring at me every time I walk into my bedroom."

"How do you reason that you need sugar then?"

"Motivation, dude! It takes effort, and effort needs sugar. More specifically, if I can be so damn rude, it needs a glass of cola."

I pour us each a glass with ice, walking across to the fridge to put it away and taking out a large cake stand, on which sits an iced black magic cake. I bring it out to him with two little plates and a knife.

"I've already offered you a drink, so that isn't rude you asking for a glass. And if you need sugar then this is one damn good fix if I do say so myself." I smile as I cut myself a slice.

"Fine. But only cause you won't let me say no." He acquiesces.

"I will let you say no, but you also said that you need sugar. I am giving you sugar. Make up your mind!" I cut him a slice as well, and we sit and eat, watching the tide.

The next day, I head to school after cooking myself some breakfast and locking up the house. As I walk along the beach path, I sing along to myself, safe in the knowledge that nobody can hear me.

"*You are what you are, I don't matter to anyone, but Hollywood legends, will never grow old, and all of what's hidden, well it will never grow cold…*"

The path doubles back on itself below the cliffs, coming down along the beach to the bay. "*But I lost myself, when I lost you, and I still got jazz, when I've got those blues, I lost myself, and I lost you too, and I still get trashed, darling, when I hear your tunes…*"

The song comes to a crescendo of a bridge, and I fall back against the rocks, up to the wall. "*I put the radio on, hold you tight in my mind, isn't strange that you're not here with me, I'm putting all the lights on, in the television, trying to transmit, can you hear me? Ground control to Major Tom, can you hear me all night long? Ground control to Major Tom…*"

I finish the vocals, and I hum the last notes to myself as I walk up to the school just as the bell rings. Slipping into my class, the Drama teacher looks at me surprised.

"Well Aidan, you're just as quiet as usual; I didn't hear you come in."

"Shouldn't you be used to that, miss?" I take out my books and uncap a pen to add to my ongoing project of a short piece that we have to perform at the end of the week, be it dance, singing or theatre. I'm singing a piece that I believe will show off my voice, which I try to hone and keep warmed up.

As she issues instructions to us with regards to our pieces, I focus on my work: the conception of my performance, and my presentation I must do for it. *I chose this performance because... I decided to perform it in this way because...* Questions fill my mind and I answer them the best I can, with my knowledge of the background of the piece showing by the detail I go into.

The room suddenly becomes warm, and I feel rather faint. I ask to be excused in order to get a drink of water, but I don't make it to the door. Rising from my seat, I get hit by a dizzy spell, feel my blood pressure drop, and crash to the floor unconscious.

# CHAPTER I

*I*t's a stormy night, just like always. All around me is noise, the sound of the thunder, of the rain, of my own heavy, ragged breathing. I realise that someone stands before me, a tall, powerful, masculine figure who, for reasons unknown, sends a shiver down my spine. I'm afraid of this man, and I don't know why.

He strikes me across my face, and I wince, but I don't protest; I know that if I do I will be deemed imperfect, unworthy. He steps on my chest, pushing me down into the ground, and I let out a strangled cry.

The rain gets in my eyes, and when I blink it away, the man is gone. I feel a pair of arms around me, raising me off the ground. The strength with which the person lifts me is great, but when I turn the silhouette I see is that of a female.

Her voice is warm and kind, like that of a sympathetic motherly figure. "Listen not to him. He is afraid. He sees you as you are, and what you are is filled with loving fire. You are strong and you have a desire in you to do what is good. Never lose your drive, young one."

*I want to reach out to her, to fall into her arms and to be protected, but she flinches at a noise. The woman turns and runs away, and my vision fades to black.*

I wake up, gasping for air, and I look around to see that I am in the school office. A glass of water is on the table next to me, and I drink it as Ben walks in.

"You alright? I heard you collapsed in Drama."

"Yeah, I overheated. It's happened before, don't worry about it." I try to reassure him that this is normal, but the thing that haunts me is that it isn't. Yes, I did overheat before, combined with low blood pressure, but this was neither of those. When you dehydrate, you get headaches, yet here I was writing as usual, no problems, then I drop to the floor.

"That won't stop me from worrying, man, I worry about you anyway. I'm the one who always offers to stay the night if you want me to, who tells you that if you need anything just holler."

"And I know that." I raise my hands. "But I can take care of myself. Thank you, but I'm fine. I have been since I came here, and I'll get by."

He sits down next to me, and lays a hand on my shoulder. "As long as you do tell me the instant something else like this happens."

"Deal." I get up, drain the remaining water from the glass, and head back to my class.

"Wait, where are you going?"

"I need to finish my work." I turn away from him, but I can still hear his good-natured protests.

It's the last day before the half term holiday, so we have a week off starting on Monday, and as I walk to work in the evening I ponder my dream.

It's just like all the others, but different at the same time. It's always been stormy, and I remember seeing nothing but silhouettes, but there was more clarity in the classroom; the man who attacked me was a giant, towering above me and having to bend low to strike me. But I don't know what I did! I don't know where I went wrong...or how I angered him enough to physically attack me. And then the woman...

She was how I imagine my mother to be, protective of her child and wanting to do anything in her power to help. Yet she didn't directly help me, she only entered when the man had gone. To fix what he had done, as if she had no power over him, and she knew that he would object if she tried to save me; she instead consoled me afterwards. But then she fled, scared by something I couldn't perceive. Maybe the man came back? Or he threatened her, so she had to leave, or else she would bear his rage?

Her exact reasons are unclear, but I understand that she loved me. She cared about me deeply, otherwise why would she offer kind words to me and help me after the attack?

Then there's the question of their identities. Who were they? My instinct tells me that they were my biological parents, but I'm not sure. Why would such a kind, benevolent woman fall for such a controlling, angry man? Maybe he charmed her in their youth, but the relationship turned sour when I was born? I don't know, but I certainly want to find out.

When I get to work, I greet my boss, Tom, and fill up the sink with warm soapy water. As I wash the dishes, he calls to me. "So how's life alone?" he smirks.

"There's not much to say, it's how it always has been. I get by." I smile to myself, "We busy today?"

"Not that busy, we had the lunch rush but we've slowed down now. You're lucky you're in when you are, Cynthia almost cried earlier."

"Aww, why?" I'm rather fond of Cynthia, she's a good friend and we both share a love of singing.

"Her boyfriend broke up with her, that and she's struggling with coursework and the fact that we were busy didn't help." Tom tells me.

"Has she left already?"

"No, she's just getting her coat and then she's off, why?"

"Would you mind if I sat down and had a chat with her?"

"'Course not, lad, maybe you'll get some."

He winks at me, and I laugh. "Oh sure. She may be gorgeous, but I don't think that I'm her type."

"And how do you figure that?"

"Because we're two different people." I turn to see Cynthia walk into the kitchen, coat in hand. "You okay?"

"I'm coping." She hugs me, and I pour us both a drink. "How's things?"

"They're good." We sit down opposite each other.

"Tom told me you got upset earlier?"

"Yeah… It all just hit me, you know? The stress of being at work, my coursework not being good enough, and my boyfriend breaking up with me..."

"And that's understandable. Sweetheart, you don't have to hide anything from us. All of us who work here with you, we're your friends as well as your colleagues." I take her free hand across the table and hold it. "And you know that I'll always be here if you want to talk."

She smiles. "Sure. You're one of the only people I can trust around here, Aidan."

"See? There's that smiling face we know and love. Now go on, get yourself home." I stand up and take our cups over to the sink.

**17**

Cynthia brushes her long blonde hair behind her, and turns to leave. "I'll see you both later." She blows me a kiss, and I return it with a friendly wink.

As soon as she's out the door, Tom turns to look incredulously at me. "You've pulled, lad."

"Have I bollocks, we both know that we're just friends." I retort, and he smirks again.

After work, I get back home and set a bowl of stew to reheat; I eat watching the sunset from the back garden, and retire to bed after hastily finishing my homework. But when I fall asleep, my dreams plague me.

*The stormy night continues. I am struck again and again by the man. He's angry, just like last time. And just like last time, I'm helped back to my feet by the woman. She offers kind words to me, but again she hears something and leaves, scared.*

*But this time, the dream continues. I see a third silhouette, and it drifts over to me as if floating. This person takes my hand and does what the woman did not; he hugs me, giving me a warm feeling of safety and protection—of comfort. I recognise him as a man, a boy even, of my own stature. He looks me in the eyes, and his voice is just as kind as his gesture.*

**18**

"I know it hurts. He hurt me, too. Just remember that I'm always with you. I'm always by your side. And when the time comes, He will never hurt any of us again. He'll see where He went wrong. I know it." He hugs me again, and I do what is most humiliating in my own eyes; I start to cry.

Don't get me wrong, if someone else is upset I'll offer them sympathy. I'll even encourage them to let it all out and to cry if they need to. But if it's me, I will never let myself cry in front of others. It makes me feel weak, as if I'm begging for sympathy. And that's not me, it's not the sort of guy I am. If anyone other than me is crying, I'll offer them sympathy. But I judge myself with a harsher punishment than other people; I beat myself up about meaningless little things. And I need to work on that.

But I'm crying in front of this guy, and He's hugging me, and telling me it's okay. "Aidan, you don't have to hide anything from us. We're your friends," He says, and I realise that it mirrors what I said to Cynthia earlier. A chill runs down my spine, and the boy continues. "Come on, we need to get back in. Otherwise he won't be happy with us, or with me for helping you. He's already taking his anger out on her, I'm lucky to have got away." He looks down, upset. "The others never had to put up with this, they're perfect." He catches me looking concerned, and brightens up. "But, all we can do is put on a happy face. Because it's okay. We get to put things right."

19

*His putting a positive spin on things inspires me, and I follow him back inside. My vision then fades again, and I'm pulled back out of my dream.*

Waking up on Saturday morning, I notice that something isn't right. I look around, and everything is as it should be. So why do I feel so uneasy?

I take a look out of my window, and I put on my dressing gown to head outside. I see a distant light and it isn't the sun, for it comes from the west, from the sea. Walking down to the part of the beach that can be reached from my house, I try and get a better look at the light. It's a shooting star, like a beacon, shining in the darkness, and it almost calls to me. If I concentrate, I can just make out a noise.

*Aaaaaa…Aaaaaaiiiii….*

It's harmonious, like singing. The light starts to come closer.

*Aaaaaaiiiii…daaaaaaannnnnn…*

Oh god. I'm hearing my name.

*Aidan!*

A chill hits me, and the light comes closer still, but it's speeding towards me. I start to run, but I catch my dressing gown on a rock. Loosening it, I see the light angle sharply upwards, and it flies over my house, missing it entirely, before curving around and coming back like a boomerang. I shield my face and dive into a gap in the rock, and what I realise is a miniature comet, no bigger that I am, flies past me, impacting in the sand.

# CHAPTER II

Okay, so maybe I didn't make the best landing.

The guy saw me, and he started to run away the further I got. In retrospect I should have just aimed for the beach to start with, but I thought maybe he wouldn't see me. So I shouted his name, and he got scared for some reason. I mean, everyone likes the sound of their name, right? I'm thankful for mine.

Anyway, I tried to change direction, so I went past his house and back down to the sand, and I just missed hitting the guy! I ought to be more careful...

So I came down onto the sand, and as the smoke cleared, I got a good look at the guy. He's the same as I remember, and he's got a sweet face, great blue eyes, and his clothes! I only wish I could choose what to wear, rather than just wearing white. Because he's wearing a massive sweeping nightgown—I think they're called that—with a greenish-blue undershirt. It looks like thin material though, does the nightgown, so he must be cold in winter! That said, he could probably wrap it around himself like a cocoon, it's that big. And the guy's only slender.

Speaking of which, he looks terrified. I probably should have made a subtler entrance...

I open my mouth to speak, but he takes several panicked steps back, onto the rocks. "Whatever you are, don't come closer. Please."

His voice as well! I swear to Lucifer, everything about him is exactly the same! "It's okay, I--"

He screams. I do not like the sound of him screaming.

"Sssh, it's okay!"

I try to reassure him, and he does stop shouting, but he's still scared of me. How could anyone be scared of me? I'm harmless! All of us are!

"It's okay. Please, don't get angry. I don't want to hurt you."

"Then who are you? And if I may be so...bold, *what* are you? You look like a human, but...the comet...and the light..." He pauses, but then his face flares up again. "AND MY NAME! Who are you?!"

I raise my hands in surrender. "I don't want to hurt you." I repeat. "I just want to speak with you. Now if *I* may be so bold, may we go inside? It's rather breezy out here, and your nightgown will only keep you so warm."

24

He fixes me with an unreadable gaze, but he acquiesces. He leads me up the sand to his house, his nightgown trailing behind him and becoming sandy. I notice that he walks with poise; he holds his shoulders back, and his head high. He knows that he belongs here, he's at home, so to speak.

We walk up the steps and into his house, where he pulls up a chair at his table. "Please excuse me, I need to go and change into something more appropriate."

"It's fine if you stay in that. I like your nightgown."

He looks confused. "Do you?"

"Yep. It's gorgeous." I reach out to touch the thin material, and it's softer than I thought. "I wouldn't be surprised if you can just swaddle yourself up in that at night." I say.

"Oh. Thanks, I guess." He crosses to the kettle, and takes a mug out of a cupboard. "Would you like a drink?"

"No, thank you."

"You sure? I'm making one, so it's no trouble."

"If you're having one, then I take my coffee black, with two sugars, please."

"Great." He smiles for the first time, and it's a genuine, winning smile, rather than a sarcastic smile that smacks of intolerance. As he makes me a drink, and himself a hot chocolate, he whistles to himself. I recognise the tune, but I refrain from singing, as it would probably irritate him further.

Mugs in hand, he pivots on one foot and hands me my coffee. "Thank you."

"It's not a problem." He takes his seat. "So first of all, who are you? And again, if I may ask, what are you?"

"First of all, can I get you to swear that you won't completely freak out when I tell you this? And that you'll listen to what I have to say first then make a decision?"

"Okay then."

"First of all, my name is Noah."

"It's a pleasure." He extends his hand to shake mine, and he has a firm, warm grip.

"If I can ask you a question, what do you expect me to say?"

"What do you mean?"

"You asked me what I am. What do you think I am?" He's silent for a few seconds, and he closes his eyes.

"I think you're some kind of intelligent life form from another solar system." He pauses, then adds, "And I very much hope you come in peace." He laughs nervously.

I smile. "That's a good guess. But first, I'm not that intelligent, and second, of course I come in peace. No, I'm actually here for you. That's why you heard your name earlier. I called to you."

His eyes widen, and he stutters slightly. "You knew who I was? How?"

"I've been watching you for a while. Ever since you came here, I've been watching you. Watching over you."

"Like, what, you're my guardian angel or something?"

"Yes."

He stops. "What?"

"Yes, I am."

His pupils dart around as he tries to figure out what I mean. "You...you are my guardian angel?"

"Yes."

He looks me dead in the eyes, drains his mug of hot chocolate, and stands up. "Bollocks."

Okay, now I'm confused. "What?"

"That's absolute rubbish! You're not... But wait, if you came down in a... And then you called to me... And... Oh my god, you are...aren't you?"

"Yes. I'm one hundred percent, swear to Lucifer, your guardian angel."

He sits back down, hands shaking, and puts them on the table to ground himself. "Heh. You swear to

Lucifer, rather than to…the guy upstairs." He corrects himself.

"Yeah, I do. We all do. I'm surprised you've noticed that."

"Thanks."

I rise from the chair. "I still have to tell you why. I've told you who I am, and what I am, but you don't know why I am here."

"Okay, tell me."

"First, you have work today. So we'll talk later." I smile, and usher him upstairs to change out of his nightclothes. "I'll be waiting when you get back, so until then have a good day."

"Oh. Okay, thanks…Noah."

"You're welcome."

He ascends to his room, nightgown trailing behind him, and I sit down in the lounge, head in my hands, wondering how I can break this news to him.


Several hours later, Aidan returns from the café, and I meet him at the beach. "Hey."

"Hi. I honestly thought you'd gone." he admits.

"I would only leave if there's no reason to stay. And if you are the reason I came here, then logically I shouldn't go."

28

He blinks. "That's a very good point." He starts to walk up to his house, but I stop him.

"I thought we could take a walk along the beach, and talk about it as we go. Or I could buy you dinner."

Aidan's expression is one of sheer disbelief, which then settles to acquiescence. "Guess I should expect kind gestures from my guardian."

"Yep. And I'm not gonna back down, so get used to it, I'm taking you for a meal, dude!" I walk up to his house, and gesture for him to go inside. "Do you want a change of clothes, or are you alright as you are?"

"I need to change out of my work clothes, so yeah I'll go get a fresh set." He ascends the stairs again, and I subtly follow him. I take in the top floor; his bedroom and a bathroom make up the second story of the house. He's rummaging in his wardrobe, and pulls out two shirts, one black and the other navy. He holds each of them up to his chest, and turns to me. "You choose."

"Black; it'll accentuate your skin and make you shine."

He chuckles, and returns the navy shirt to the wardrobe. "You have a way with words, my friend."

I blush. "Thanks."

He finishes buttoning up his shirt, and changes into a pair of navy chinos with black Chuck Taylors. "Are you going to change? Or can you change clothes?"

"I can, and I will. Excuse me." I enter his bathroom, and return wearing a white shirt and pale grey trousers, coupled with white plimsolls.

He looks me up and down, and again I am faced with that cute smile. "You and I seem like total opposites, what could you possibly want with me?"

"Only from your colour scheme. You're very much like me, in terms of personality, conduct, that sort of thing."

He nods to me, a *'can't argue with that'* sort of gesture. "Shall we go, then?"


Aidan leads me through town, to a quaint Italian restaurant overlooking the other side of the beach, and from where I can see the waves striking the sand. It's all very serene.

A slender, pretty waitress takes us to our table, and I glance at the menu, ordering a glass of water and a cola for myself and Aidan, along with a garlic bread to share. I catch him looking out across the sea, and I take in the view.

The sun is just setting, and I can see a murmuration of starlings soaring overhead. We both watch them fly, and they appear to split into two groups before reforming. They then fly directly over the café as one group again.

Aidan picks up his glass with a smile. "Cheers." He and I toast our glasses, before he continues. "So why are you here, Noah?"

"Well, to tell you the truth, I'm here for you."

"We've established that, but why me? Of all people, you choose me?"

"Yeah. And that's because of what happened here last year."

He stops mid-drink, and his eyes go wide. "What do you know about what happened last year?" His voice drops.

"I can't tell you al--"

"Then tell me what you can. Please. I... I need to know." His expression becomes one of sorrow, and I instantly feel bad.

"Alright. You know how I'm your guardian angel?"

"Just about."

"Well the reason I took that role was because I had to keep you safe after what happened that lead up to your memory loss. I knew you way back when, before the...incident, and you haven't changed a bit. You're just as passionate and fiery as always." I smile at him.

"Thank you, I guess." He laughs softly. "People do say that I need to give myself a break sometimes, they say I'm too determined to push myself and to handle too much."

**31**

"You always were." I repeat. "The incident wiped your memory clean, but I think that the...person responsible, may have missed a few things."

"What do you mean, missed a few things?"

"They intended to give you total amnesia, but some memories must have survived." I word my sentences carefully, to avoid Aidan getting the wrong idea.

"Well if they intended amnesia, then they got it. All I remembered when I woke up on that beach, and when Ben found me, was my name."

I take his hand across the table on impulse, and I can tell he's surprised. "But they left more. You still have memories. Please try to think, what else do you remember from your past life?"

"I don't, Noah. I don't know any--" He stops, and I study his face carefully.

His expression goes through several swift changes, as if he's trying to remember something, or as if he knows what he wants to say but can't figure out how to word it. "Wait. There is something."

"Go on."

"When you get retrograde amnesia, you can sometimes retrieve those memories through dreams or flashbacks. And I think it has to do with the stuff I dream, my dreams always come back to the same

32

thing. I just see a stormy night, black clouds all around me, and all I can hear is thunder.

"That said, yesterday afternoon I fainted in class and had another dream, but it was different. There was more."

"More? What do you mean?"

He looks at me, now studying my face as I had his before he continues. "Like, I saw a huge man standing in front of me. He was attacking me, hitting me over and over, and then he was gone and there was another, a woman, who helped me up and told me not to listen to him, that everything was fine, that I'd done nothing wrong."

"What did she look like?" I lean forwards ever so slightly.

"I didn't see her face, just a silhouette, but she had the most beautiful voice." A faraway look crosses his face. "It was how I imagine silk to sound."

"I know what you mean. It's beautiful, her voice."

"Yeah, it--" He stops. "What?"

"Her voi--" I gasp as I realise the implications of my words.

"You know the woman from my dreams?"

*Oh, shit.* I swallow. *No turning back now.* "I do. I know what happened."

His face switches from anger at me not telling him, to sheer joy at finally being able to know. "Then please! Tell me!" he stutters.

The waitress brings our meals to the table, and I ask for refills of our drinks. When she brings them, I thank her and start to tell Aidan the truth.

"I knew you before your accident. I've always known you. Your name is Aidan, you take the form of a seventeen-year-old, as do I."

"So the man I saw, do you know him as well?"

"I… I regret to say I do."

"Is he my father?"

"You could say that. And the woman…she's like your mother. And I'm like your brother. We're not directly related, but we all grew up together."

"Wait, how can we have grown up together? You've said that you're my guardian angel."

"Well, we grew up…upstairs."

As my words sink in, I take a swig of my water and start on my lasagne. I try and focus on the taste of the food, rather than worrying about Aidan's reaction. The pasta sheets have some bite to them, and the meaty flavour comes through beautifully.

"So…you're trying to tell me…that I'm an *angel*?"

"Yes. We grew up in Heaven."

His face turns to stone. He stands up, and glares at me. "You're lying."

"No, I'm not. Aidan. I'm unable to lie, I'm a perfect being. So I can only act in the most loving way.

Lying isn't a loving act."

"But…even so, you're… I'm not an angel. That's ridiculous."

"You are. And if I have to prove it to you, then I will."

"Ugh…!" He lets out what I can only describe as a growl, and reluctantly sits back down. "I'm sorry. This is…just… It's difficult, you know? And, I guess beggars can't be choosers, I'm getting the only explanation to my past and I'm just refuting it."

"I know it's hard. It's always going to be difficult hearing something you don't believe, and trying desperately to comprehend it in a way that softens the blow. To either normalise it, or make it out to be just a delusion.

"But I'll explain everything to you. I swear to Lucifer that I'll be with you throughout all of this. If you'll let me."

He sighs deeply. "Okay. Thank you, man."

"You're very welcome." I smile, and take his hand across the table. "It'll be okay. I'll explain it all. And as I say, I'll prove it if that's what you need."

"I'd prefer it." He offers me a weak smile.

"It's no trouble. But if it's all the same, can I explain it later?"

"Sure. For now, let's just enjoy this."

I nod, taking more forkfuls of lasagne, and I catch the waitress' eye. She beams at me. "You're so cute!" she mouths.

Aidan must have seen her, for he almost chokes on his tagliatelle, and I smirk.

# CHAPTER III

After our meal, we order a chocolate brownie to share, and as I pass the waitress on our way out she whispers to me. "Congratulations."

I smile, and glance across to Aidan, who's already off back to his house. I catch up with him. "What's up?"

"Not much, just waiting for you to spill."

"Spill?" I don't know the term.

"Yeah, to tell me what's happened, what's on your mind. What you said you'd tell me back there, but didn't."

I feel guilty. "Okay. Do you want to stop and talk, or should we keep walking?"

"We can stop down at the beach below my house." We walk further along, and I see that the crater I made this morning has disappeared due to the waves pushing the sand into it all day. Aidan perches on a large rock, and I sit down adjacent to him.

"What do you want to know?"

"First, what was life like up there?"

"Oh, it was glorious. We would just watch over the world, keeping track of everything and ensuring that everything ran smoothly. A girl auditioned for a musical in Copenhagen, I ensured that the judge was honest with his critique. She passed. We're pretty much the voice of conscience, and we angels all each embody virtues. We have anger, joy, patience, comfort, compassion and bravery, among plenty of others.

"That said, sometimes we can't change minds so easily. A school shooting in Oregon, a failed attempt at a guilt trip. Rather literally." I smile sadly. "That was a tough day, for all of us."

"So you have a virtue that is yours uniquely?"

"Yep. We all balance our virtues, but there's one that stands out for each of us, and that's our Core. My Core, for example, is comfort. I help others when they're feeling down."

"That's sweet."

"You had one, as well. You embodied bravery. You stood up when nobody else did. You hated the idea of injustice."

"Still do." Aidan replies with a smile.

"And that makes me so darn happy to see. The fact that you'll never settle for anything less than what is right. You're brave as all Heaven."

"Thank you. But it's not that difficult here, we

have an acting society at school, and I sing in the school choir, so it's not that big of a deal."

"Rubbish. Aidan, that takes courage, to sing and act in front of others. It takes a hell of a lot. To put yourself out there and allow yourself to be judged by your peers, it's a brave move."

"If you say so."

"Which I do. What's next on your list of things you want to know?"

"Who were the man and the woman? Was the man God? And if so, what relevance is the woman to him?"

"That will have been Yahweh. That's His actual name, but it's interchangeable."

"And the woman?"

"That's Asherah, or the Goddess. Some call Her Mother, or the Lady, but I prefer to call Her by Her name, it seems more majestic than any of those titles."

"So, if She's a Goddess--"

"*The* Goddess."

"The Goddess, sorry, then does that mean that She's Go-- Yahweh's...wife?"

"You could see it like that. Or you could just see them as equal beings, rather than joined in matrimony."

"So Yahweh and Asherah are like the Lord and Lady of Heaven?"

"Exactly."

"Okay. So where do I come in?"

"I was getting to that." I absentmindedly pick up a small pebble, turning it over in my hand. "I have to take you and bring you back to Heaven."

I attempt to be calm, but my voice quivers as I break the news. I see his face fall. "You mean I'd have to…leave? Leave here?"

I nod curtly. "Yes. And I know that it'd be difficult, but I really need--"

"No. I'm sorry, Noah, but I'm not going with you."

"Aidan, please listen to me. You have the right to know why."

"It's because I need to be punished, isn't it? My dreams involved Yahweh attacking me for doing wrong, being imperfect."

"He did attack you. But that's not why we need you. You used to be an angel. You were cast out of Heaven by Yahweh, and it was His will that you woke up on the beach with no memories."

"I know that. You've told me that."

"Do you know *why*?"

He pauses, looking out over the waves. The sun is just on the horizon, setting as we speak. A faint breeze ripples through his hair, and his faraway gaze makes him look full of majesty. "I'm guessing it's because I'm different. Because I thought differently to the others, because I'm so passionate about justice."

"You're partly right. You defied Yahweh. You questioned His omnibenevolence, and His omnipotence."

"His what?"

"He's meant to be all-powerful, or omnipotent. He's also meant to be omnibenevolent, which means all-loving. He loves every one of us to the highest extent anyone can love them. He would do anything for us."

"But if he would do anything for us, and he has the power to do anything for us…"

"Then why do evil and suffering exist?" I complete his sentence. "And that is what you asked Yahweh. You asked Him why bad things happen, and what the good people in this world did to deserve the horrors that they witness."

"Sounds like me to be honest." He laughs good-naturedly.

I smile. "Anyway, the point is that Yahweh couldn't answer that question. You cornered Him, and a cornered animal is the most dangerous. He was really brutal towards you for questioning Him, and just as He cast Lucifer out, so did He you. But you were so innocent about it. You went about it in just the right way; you softened the blow as much as was possible. And still He snapped at you.

"I think it was because Lucifer questioned him all those years ago, and now He effectively had a second Lucifer in the form of you."

"So…I'm the Devil, Part Two?"

"No. You're just the second to question Him. Lucifer was the first, and he is the one and only Devil. Yahweh cast Him all the way down to the Inferno, and he was relatively lenient with you, only sending you to the mortal realm. So you got off lightly."

"Guess so." He says, relieved. "But then why do I have to go back?"

"Because you sent Yahweh into a spiralling insecurity. He could handle Lucifer, because He was just one. But you're a special case. Lucifer was always rebellious, whereas you were brave, and in being brave you had the courage to stand up and question the truth. You were just like the rest of us, kind and virtuous in every way. You were one of the 'normal' angels. And if a 'normal' angel could question, then what's to stop all of us questioning, and then, by extension, a rebellion of Paradise?"

"I can see where you're coming from." He picks up a pebble, and skims it across the waves.

"So He banished you to make you a modern-day

example. 'How you are fallen from Heaven, O Lucifer, son of the morning! How you are cut down to the ground, You who weakened the nations!' That said, Lucifer wanted to be the ruler of Heaven, he wanted to be the most powerful. You did no such thing, or even implied any such thing. So you were essentially, to use your phrase, the straw that broke the camel's back."

I toss my pebble up in the air, catch it, and skim it across the waves. "Anyway, we need you because Asherah is deeply worried. The Lady is afraid of Yahweh; He's become angry, frightening and vengeful, like back in the Old Testament days. He Himself has caused so much pain and suffering that we're struggling to rectify it all. We angels are using our Cores to help those affected, and Asherah is doing Her best any way She can, but we can only do so much against Him. In the wake of all this chaos, Her mind has turned to you, and She views that you coming back and repenting will solve the problem."

I watch his face. Several minutes later, he hasn't spoken. "Aidan?"

"Yeah?"

"Are you okay?"

"No. Because…if I go with you, then I'll have to leave my family here."

"Aidan, we are your family."

"No you're not!" he roars. "You're nothing like me! You're perfect! You're virtuous, and kind, and everything you said! I'm so pathetic, I get stressed and scared and I fall behind. I do my best but my best isn't good enough! I could never fit in with you, with your perception of family. My real family is the people I've lived with here, the ones who've welcomed me in, who've made me feel like I'm...home."

I'm shocked. I never expected an outburst. But I suppose bravery does include standing up to your friends, and telling them how you feel. I stand up, and lay a hand on his shoulder. "It's alright. I shouldn't have said that, I understand how you feel. I won't make you go if you don't want to. But I'll hang around for a few days, if that's okay? Just if you change your mind?"

He nods after a few seconds debating, and I see his eyes shining. *Must just be the sunset*, I think. "Okay. I have a sofa-bed, so you can sleep in my bed and I'll take the sofa."

"That's gracious of you, but I'll take downstairs. You've been so kind in just putting up with all of this and not getting angry before now."

We walk back to his house, and as I get settled down to sleep downstairs, I swear that I can hear Aidan crying.

# CHAPTER IV

*T*he storm rages on overhead. Asherah runs away from me, and the third person comes to my aid. I recognise their voice. It's sweet, and harmonious, pleasing to my ears. It resonates rather like that of Asherah, and he helps me up.

*"All we can do is put on a happy face. Because it's okay. We get to put things right." He and I start to walk back, and I turn to face him, but I still see nothing but shadow.*

*That's okay, because it's normal. I never see their faces. I feel his hand take mine, and I give his a gentle squeeze. Looking up at him, I smile. He stops to embrace me again, but something in the background makes me flinch. I think I saw something moving, but I'm not sure what. I stop, looking around whilst still holding on to his hand.*

*But it's suddenly ripped away from mine; I turn to him and he's falling away from me, grabbed and thrown away in the darkness. I'm grasped by an iron fist, and I'm pulled off the ground.*

As I choke, I can see that the boy is being tended to by Asherah, and it's Yahweh who is gripping my neck. I desperately try to prise His fingers away, and my voice comes out as a raspy drawl. "Please…"

"Why do you persist?! Why do you keep trying to taint that which is good and virtuous?" His voice is booming, a cacophony assaults my eardrums and I think they're about to break.

"I didn't mean to! Please forgive me!" I beg, tears streaming down my face, but He does not listen. He slams me onto the ground, and leans close to my face.

"You're a vicious little brute, aren't you? Far from the brave being you once were. You dare to think I am not powerful enough? I will break you. I will show to you that I have power enough to silence those who dare to doubt me."

His fingers loosen from my neck, and He creates a sphere of light in His hand, which He uses to blind me. I shield my eyes, and I feel His foot connect with my stomach, hurling me down through the ground and emerging on the other side. I see myself falling down, down into the abyss. Into the pit from which nothing can escape. I try to reach out, to grasp some kind of anchor that will keep me safe, but to no avail. I keep falling, and all around me I see nothing but black.

And one thing that comes to me later is the fact that, as Yahweh reprimanded me, a dusting of snow began to fall.

I wake up in my bed with a shout.

Noah bolts up the stairs, and is by my side in an instant. "What happened? Are you okay?"

My breaths come out heavy and ragged. "Yeah. Yeah, I'm fine. Just a bad dream."

"Another flashback?"

"I think so. I saw Asherah again, She ran away, and the other person came, they comforted me. But then Yahweh grabbed me, and... Noah, I think I saw my Fall..."

"What do you mean?"

"I mean, I saw Yahweh cast me out from Heaven. I saw myself being kicked through the ground, and I fell through the air into the pit."

"The pit? You mean... the Inferno?" His voice is disbelieving.

"Not necessarily. I didn't see any fire, or anything like that, I just saw darkness."

"It seems that He chose a different path for you. Either He didn't intend for you to go through Purgatory and the Inferno, or He was so consumed by rage that He didn't care where you went." Noah sits down on the bed, thinking, and I take a drink of water to calm myself.

"Thank Go--*Yahweh* it's Sunday." I correct myself.

"You're getting the hang of it." Noah smiles. He

then returns to his cogitative position. I rise from my bed, put on my dressing gown and walk down to the kitchen, the carpet soft and welcoming against my feet. I grab a small wok, eggs, sugar and flour, and crack on with making pancakes for myself and Noah.

He comes down swiftly afterwards, dressed in his nightclothes—a pale grey t-shirt and checked grey-and-white bottoms. "You don't have to cook for me, I ca--"

"No, I'm cooking." I interrupt him. "You're the guest, I would never make you cook."

"I would be volunteering to cook…" he remarks, before reluctantly sitting at the table. I hand him a plate of pancakes and a fork, place glasses of water on the table, after which I serve myself and switch off the hob. "Isn't there anything else you want to know about your dream?"

"Not particularly. I honestly try, and have tried for the past year, to put them to the back of my mind, forget about them." I have a drink of my water. "But I can't do this now, it seems." I cast Noah a glance as if to say, *you won't let me forget, will you?*

"No you can't. It's important, Aidan. You can't avoid this, so the best thing to do would be to accept it and say you'll go back to Heaven with me." he says resignedly.

*So that's it then. I do have to leave.* I look down, and

**48**

Noah sighs. "When you put it like that…I don't have a choice, do I?" I ask.

Noah avoids my gaze. He's dodging the question because he knows I'm right. "No." he says finally.

I get up, put our crockery, cutlery and the wok in the sink and wash them up, all the while refraining from speaking. I'm scared, I'll admit it. I don't want to go with Noah, because I'm scared to leave all of my friends behind. I'm a very sociable and friendly person, if I do say so myself, and one of my biggest flaws is that I always blame myself for any little thing that upsets anyone else.

I have this stupid mind-set that I'm somehow everything to everyone, and that my actions will affect everyone in my wider social circle, even those I've only met once. So as I'm standing here mind-numbingly washing up, I'm thinking about the tiny implications of my actions to the most separated individual who knows me, like that one girl I never speak to in my class, or that customer who asks after me on Sundays when I have my day off.

It's daft, really, and I need to work on it. Noah, however, interprets this as me giving him the silent treatment, and he suddenly bursts out. "Please! Say something, Aidan!" After a few moments, he adds desperately, "Anything…"

I turn to look him in the eyes. "There's nothing to

say. You've told me that I have to go with you."

"Well...you can say no, but I can't say that Asherah will give up that easily. She could send more angels to get you and take you back, and compared to some of the others, you've got off lightly in me coming to get you." He glances around the room but I walk straight over to him, forcing him to look at me.

"I know what you're doing, Noah. You're trying to guilt trip me into coming with you, aren't you?"

He stays silent.

"Aren't you?" I ask with a bit more force.

"And what if I am? Is it working? Does it make you want to come with me, out of your own choice rather than obligation?" His tone is bitter, and it doesn't suit him.

"Well imagine if you were living a perfectly good life, then someone swept through it like a fucking hurricane, told you that you weren't really who you thought you were, and then gave you veiled orders to come with them. How would you feel?" I snap. "That's the choice you're having me make. And it hurts."

Following this remark, I head out the door. I can hear Noah get up. "Where are you going?"

I fix him with a glare. "Anywhere to get away from this." I gesture to everything around me, before shutting the door.

As soon as I leave the house, I instinctively start for the town. I try to find something, anything to take my mind off things. I settle on a drink at work, so I make for the café. I see Cynthia working, and she gives me a smile and a wave.

"Hey, Aidan, what can I get you?"

"A hot chocolate please, Cyn, I need to calm down."

"Why? It's not even twelve yet, what's got you bothered?"

I sit down as she brings me the drink. "Just...I'm frustrated. It's like I've got a weight on my shoulders that I can't shake."

"Well doesn't singing help you relax? I remember you saying that you're most at peace when you walk along the beach and just sing to the ocean."

Images of Noah crash-landing flash through my mind, along with our introduction and last night's walk, and I cast them away. "No, that wouldn't help. Too many bad memories." I laugh nervously.

"Is it the sea that's bothering you?" Cynthia asks jokingly, but her tone then becomes serious. "Well if singing doesn't help, then I think you might need closure. You say it's like a weight on your shoulders, something's bugging you. Like a burden you're trying to run away from but you can't. And the worst part is

**51**

that you know you can't run from it. Yet still you try. Why?"

I wait until I finish my drink to answer her. "Because…even though I know I can't outrun this, it's come as such a shock to me that this has happened that I'm trying to get back to normality. And normality for me is to just reject what's happened and carry on with my life."

"We're back to you running away from the problem. Aidan, you need to face up to this, whatever it is, and if it means you making a difficult decision, then so be it." Cynthia gets up. "I need to get back to work, but you know where I am if you need me."

"Yeah. Thanks." I stand up, paying a tip and leaving.

With a clear mind, I go about my business in town, shopping for food to stock up for the week, dropping into the stationer's to grab a notebook, and I walk along the beach back home with bags in hand, thinking about Noah.

I have to apologise for how I acted earlier, but I need to own up to the fact that I have to go with him. It's accepting that which is so hard for me.

I open the door and back into the kitchen to put my things away, but I can tell that something isn't right. "Noah?" I call out.

52

Nothing.

After packing the food into the fridge, I go upstairs to stick the notebook in a drawer. "Noah, you up here?" Still nothing.

I wrack my brains to try to think of a reason, but its then that I see the envelope on the coffee table.

*Aidan,*

*Although this isn't the best thing for me to do, it's what you want. And who am I to stand in the way of someone else being happy?*

*By the time you read this, I'll be gone, back up to Heaven to tell Asherah that the plan failed. Yahweh will probably be angry if He finds out I've gone, but all I can do is try and bear it. It's happened before, but I'll be alright.*

*Goodbye Aidan, and I hope you have a nice life, wherever you are.*

I read the letter over and over again, and then I look down and I'm crying. A tear smudges his writing. I wipe my eyes and scan the note again for any little detail about how I can reach him, but there's nothing.

I sit down on the sofa, letter in hand, and I'm suddenly angry. Angry with him for leaving, angry with the gods for hurting us both. But most of all I'm angry with myself for pushing him away. For making him feel unwanted, making him feel like he's in the wrong for doing nothing but his job.

"You're so fucking stupid…" I tell myself. "Look

at what you've done!" More tears roll down my face, and I grab the envelope and rip it open in frustration.

Something then catches my eye about the envelope, and I open it up to a flat sheet of paper.

Words. But not just words, song lyrics.

I read through them, trying to recognise the song, and it's an old hymn. More so, it's the only hymn I know off by heart. I wonder why he would write these lyrics down, unless they're another message to me. Maybe a way to get in touch?

I take a deep breath, and begin to sing.

*O Holy Night, the stars are brightly shining, it is the night of our dear saviour's birth.*

I run outside to look out over the sea and to have a better chance of seeing Noah.

*Long lay the world, in sin and error pining, 'til he appeared, and the soul felt its worth.*

The night sky appears to gleam as I sing.

*A thrill of hope, the weary world rejoices, for yonder breaks, a new and glorious morn.*

I can just see something in the distance, by the horizon.

*Fall on your knees, O hear the angel voices. O night, divine, O night, when Christ was born. O night, divine, O night, O night divine.*

The far-off something starts to glow brightly.

*Sweet hymns of joy, in grateful chorus raise we, let all*

*within us, praise His holy name.*

The glow gets bigger, and I see that it's coming towards me fast.

*Christ is the Lord, let ever, ever praise we.*

*Noel, noel. O night, O night divine.*

I take a quick breath, and the glow streaks through the night, flying down to land gracefully on the sand.

*O night, divine, O night, O holy, night.* I belt out the last lines of the hymn, and the glow dissipates, leaving the familiar form of the angel standing on the beach.

# CHAPTER V

I run at him, grabbing him and almost knocking him off his feet. Noah bursts out laughing. "So? Did it work?"

"I'm so sorry… For everything I did. Please forgive me." I beg of him, holding him tightly.

He looks at me warmly. "It's me who should apologise. I just ran off like that without giving you a proper chance. I'm guessing you found that letter?"

"And the envelope." I nod.

"A fail-safe. In case you changed your mind." A guilty look comes over his face. "Listen, Aidan, I should never have tried to deliberately upset you or anything. The last thing I wanted was to make you feel bad. And as soon as I saw you open up the envelope and find the words, I set off straight away."

"You saw that?"

"Yeah. I'm your guardian, aren't I? I can see whatever you're doing from up there. I watch over you." He walks past me, leads me back up to my house. "I saw you cry and it...it hurt. To know that I caused that pain, it's a horrible feeling."

I open the door and let us both in, putting the kettle on. "I know what you mean. I'm usually the first to apologise for things, even things I didn't do."

"See, that takes bravery, to swallow your pride and admit your mistakes. It shows that you embody it the most out of us." Noah points out. "And not just out of you and me, out of all the Virtuous Ones, you are the bravest. None of us would ever have the...the *balls* to confront Yahweh about his role."

I pour him a mug of coffee, handing it to him as I sit down at the table. "I want you to know that I've been thinking it over, and I've..." I take a deep breath to calm my nerves. "I've decided to go with you. Back up to Heaven to set things right..."

"Thank you."

"...on one condition."

"Which is?" Noah looks at me with concern.

"That I can come back here after things are sorted. Because I think what I've been most afraid of has been to leave here for the foreseeable future. And never being able to properly say goodbye. So the best I can do is return when it's finished."

The concerned look is replaced with a broad smile. "That's good enough for me. I'm sure that once

He sees that you're remorseful, He'll accept your apology."

"Thanks." I finish my glass of water that I poured myself, and stand up. "Can I get you anything to eat? I'll assume we're not leaving immediately?"

"We can wait a few days for you to say goodbye, but then we need to go."

"Okay. So do you want anything?"

"To be honest, anything comforting sounds really good right about now." he smiles. I cross to the fridge and take out a pan full of rice, setting it down on the bench. "What you got?"

"Well I made a batch of lemon risotto the day before you came, and it needs eating." I ladle out bowls of the sticky comfort food, putting them in the microwave. "And we have some leftover cake in the fridge as well, I could warm that up with some cream in a bit if you want?"

Noah grins. "I swear to Lucifer, Aidan, you and I are so damn similar." He pauses, then answers guiltily, "I would like that, if that's okay?"

"Sure it is. Now get yourself sat down and I'll bring it over to you."


I put on a film and we eat as the cool night sets in; the risotto has a citrus-y flavour that is refreshing and at the same time it's got some bite to it that really satisfies. It's the perfect sort of food that you can just eat after a long day and feel better, but not at all guilty, for eating.

"So I'm guessing you made this yourself?"

"Yep. Granted, the chef at work had to show me how to make it, but she's a really nice lady and gave me plenty of tips on how to do it right."

"Well how else do we learn but from example?"

"Don't ask me that, Noah." I smile. "You'll get me into a big debate about behaviourism and psychodynamics."

"Debate about what?"

"Sorry. They're psychological terms, if something is behaviourist then it's what you can see happening, like a child looking at a role model and copying their behaviour."

"Okay…"

"And if something is psychodynamic then it's what you can't see. Like the reason for a father hitting his child isn't because he's stressed, it's because he was hit as a child and it is cathartic for him to let out that anger. That's psychodynamic."

"I'm sorry I asked, that's really complicated."

"It's okay, I have a habit of going round the houses when I explain things." I finish off my risotto and take our bowls into the kitchen to load up the dishwasher, before cutting us each a decent slice of cake, which I reheat, and pouring some cream over the top. Handing Noah his bowl, I sit back down.

We eat for a few minutes, then Noah breaks the silence. "Could you say that Yahweh's treatment of us is psychodynamic? Because it relates to His insecurity?"

"You could." I realise just how much sense this makes. "Because He can't show any weakness because He's perfect, and therefore it wouldn't be behaviourist, but at the same time He's ineffable and we can't understand Him. So everything He does would be psychodynamic, cause the point of behaviourism is that you can see it happening and understand it."

Noah nods in agreement. "I get you." I take a mouthful of the cake, and the sweetness of it floods my taste buds. The rich, moist cake and the warm dark buttercream are baked well, and the cream mixes with some of the buttercream to make a deep velvety sauce.

"It's weird, how we can assign human values and attributes near perfectly to Yahweh, and yet we still call Him ineffable." I say when we finish our dessert.

"But at the same time, we both know how He really is, aside from the mortal realm of knowledge of Him."

"Well, you do."

"So do you. You know that He's insecure, vengeful, powerful, He makes snap decisions to chuck great angels out of Heaven..." Noah sits next to me. "He's not as perfect as they say. He destroyed Sodom, He flooded the world, all of these things He did out of retaliation to the humans he created. But I think it's okay for Him to not be perfect."

"Why not?"

"Cause it shows that He's just as much subject to sin as we ourselves are. It humanises Him, rather than keeping that epistemic distance."

"What distance?" I'm confused.

"Epistemic. It means a distance in knowledge between humans and immortals. Humans can only understand so much about the gods, so there's an epistemic distance because there will always be something they don't know. It's what we mean when we say that He is ineffable." Noah takes one look at my face and laughs. "It's difficult, I know."

"Don't get me started on the Holy Trinity..." I say to him. "Speaking of which, because Yahweh is part of the Holy Trinity of Father, Son and Holy Spirit, is Asherah part of a Trinity as well?"

"Nope. She's an independent goddess, rather than being three beings in the same conscious at once."

"It's weird, cause you say that... Yahweh essentially has multiple personality disorder, where all

62

three personalities are in the driving seat at once, and Asherah is like a stress ball to Him. He takes his anger out on Her, and She calms Him down." I sum things up as best I can, and Noah smiles.

"That's a very good way of looking at it. I would say I'm surprised, but I'm not, because I know how sharp you are."

"Please. Compared to a lot of others--"

"And that's another thing about you, Aidan, sorry for interrupting. You compare yourself to everyone around you far too much. You look for the flaws in yourself and tell yourself that the people who *choose to surround you* are so much better than you are, that they can do better than you, you wonder what you bring to the table compared to them. And that," he lays a hand on my shoulder, "is the worst thing you can do. It shows a lack of self-confidence."

"Well I'm not self-confident. I can't do what others can do; I'm not as smart, or athletic, or handsome as other people." I tell him.

"You're right there. But there's admitting that, and there's blowing it out of proportion and falling into the depths of self-pity. Thinking that you're nothing to people, or that you don't matter because for everything you can do there's someone who can do it better. That's not true. You're not a background character in somebody else's film, or a plot device in a book to fill up a word count, Aidan. You're your own person, you are who you are. You have plenty of ability to write *your own* story and make it as grand and as much of a masterpiece as anyone else's. So what if you can't sprint a marathon, who cares if you can't do calculus? You have personality, you have character, and you're full of what society needs more of; honesty, kindness and innocence.

"So never sell yourself short. Yahweh saw a spark in you, and that's why He made you an angel. And He wasn't wrong about you back then. Now, maybe, but when He chose us, He knew exactly what He was doing. Asherah too, She gave Him the go-ahead, and you were a special one whom She passed without a negative thought. She never doubted your ability as the Form of the Brave, and She was right to do that."

We watch the rest of the film, and as the credits roll, Noah's words resonate with me. *Never sell yourself short.* He really sees the best in everyone. I can see why Yahweh made him an angel. He's so kind, he's like that friend you always want around cause he lifts your spirit just by you looking at him. Knowing that he's there for you.

I switch off the lights, and I look out of the back doors to see that a storm is brewing. Huge dark clouds are rolling in, falling over each other like commuters on a train, each one trying to get in and to their destination first.

I close the curtains and lock us in, ensuring that nothing will fall over in the bad weather, and I'm about to make my way upstairs when Noah's voice stops me.

"Looks like a rough one. I've never liked storms. They remind me of…that night. When He…"

"When He cast me down?"

"Yeah. And that's one night I long to forget." He turns to look at me.

"Well I have to dream about it every night, so you've got it easy." I say to him with a smile. "Are you sure you don't want to sleep upstairs, and I'll take the sofa tonight?"

"I'm sure. This is your house, and I would never abuse your offer of hospitality." He wraps the throw over himself, and settles down for the night while I go up and change into my nightclothes, swathing myself in my sheets, as it's rather cold upstairs and the storm won't help in that respect.

I fall asleep and dream of thunder and lightning, but movement in my room wakes me in the night, and I turn on my bedside lamp to see that I've acquired an unexpected visitor.

Noah is lying by my side in bed, holding me and

quivering. I hear a roar of thunder and he looks up at me. "I'm sorry."

I shake my head. "Don't be. It's natural to be afraid of things. And if this comforts you, then it's a negligible price to pay." I nod off again, holding Noah gently.

When I wake, I'm alone. I wonder if last night was a dream, a departure from the stormy nights I've had to endure, but I see a depression in the mattress where Noah has laid next to me. Also, thinking about my sleep, last night was the first night I had dreamless sleep. Every other night since I came here I've dreamt, and dreamt of storms. Whereas last night when I woke in the night, I drifted off and had a night's sleep with no bad dreams.

Rising from my bed and walking downstairs, and still processing the revelation that my nightmares left me alone for once, I see Noah making us bacon and scrambled eggs, whistling as he works. He turns to me when he hears my footsteps, and his face takes on a look of guilt. "Sorry about last night. It was wrong of me."

"What do you mean?"

"I shouldn't have intruded. That's your personal space, and I got far too close. It won't happen again."

66

He gives me a plate of food and sits down opposite me, looking down in guilt.

It's awkward, eating with him when I know that I can't say anything to change his mind. It doesn't bother me though, the fact that he felt scared and wanted comfort during the storm; I have no qualms about it. It's him who is making this difficult by feeling as if he's in the wrong.

That said, the meal in front of me is more than enough of an apology. The salty bacon is just how I like, crispy without being overcooked, and in the scrambled eggs I detect a hint of cheese, adding a slight bite to the creamy texture and perfectly melding with the bacon.

I finish off my breakfast, but as soon as I finish Noah takes my utensils and plate, washing them up so I can't do it myself. This frustrates me, as I want to show him that he shouldn't go out of his way just to get me to see that he's right.

When he dries them using the tea towel on the side, before putting them away, Noah turns to see me stood there. "What do you want to do, then?"

"You said you had to say goodbye to people, right? Let's do that." he says, avoiding my eyes.

I reluctantly accept, and we walk down into town to see Cynthia at the café. As I walk, I keep replaying last night in my mind. I just woke up, and he was there, holding me as if his life depended on it. I didn't mind, and I still don't. But the question I keep asking myself is why? *Why don't I mind?*

Why don't I care that he held on to me so tightly, that he's comforted by me, that I bring him safety? After all, it's not a bad thing. And he's so sweet; he tries to do what's kind, in some cases as opposed to what's right. I decide that it isn't a bad thing to like the guy, as we seem to have become close in the few days that I've known him. Granted, in reality we've known each other for longer, I just can't remember it. But it feels as if I've known him for longer, and I guess that's what matters.

When we get to the café, it's not pleasant. Cynthia gets upset, stopping work to hug me and ask me if I'm coming back.

"Of course. I'll be back before you know it, I just need to take some time to think about things and get everything in order."

"What sort of things?"

I think carefully about how to word this. "Something resurfaced in my memory, and I need to follow it back. I don't know how long it will take, but I will come back." I tell her, which suffices.

"Let me know where you are, okay?"

"I can't guarantee that, I probably won't have signal or that, and I use social media to talk to people more than I ever text or call."

"Okay. Just…be safe, okay?"

"Sure." I embrace her again, and she smiles.

"Happy travels."

We leave the café, and turn up to head to Ben's workplace, in the northern part of town. As soon as we get there, Noah grabs the door handle and pulls it open for me, ushering me in, and I can't take it anymore.

"Okay, Noah, just stop. Please. It's driving me crazy, you beating yourself up about what happened. It's a one-time thing, you did nothing wrong, as I said. What's it gonna take to get it into your head that you're perfectly fine and that I'm not angry with you?"

"But you should be! It's wrong for me to be so close to you."

"Why?"

"Because I'm your guardian. I'm supposed to watch over you, to help you. Not the other way around."

"Noah, sometimes that's what needs to happen. When you're friends with someone, it's not because you have to be. It's because you want to be. So if you want to feel safe, then that's fine. And if sharing a bed with me makes you feel safe, then that's also fine.

People don't have assigned roles, we fluctuate. If you need comforting, you who embodies Comfort, then that's alright. And if I need courage, then I'll rely on you to help me."

He ponders it for some time, but finally acquiesces. "Alright. Sorry, I've just been being stupid today. It's funny how I was telling you last night that you shouldn't feel that everything is your fault, when now it's you telling me. The guardian has become the guarded." He smirks. He then takes the door handle again and opens it for me. "After you."

I walk in and quickly spot Ben, walking over to him. "Hey man."

"Hey, how's it going?"

"It's alright. Listen, have you got a minute? I need to tell you something."

"Hang on." He disappears into the back room, and comes back out five minutes later, during which time I look around the place. Ben works in a shop that sells e-cigarette fluids, and whilst I've never been remotely tempted to try either genuine cigarettes or e-cigarettes, the flavours of some of the liquids do interest me.

"Cherry Popper," I read, as Ben re-enters the shop floor. "Very suggestive."

He laughs. "That one was put forwards by the manager."

"Well I wonder what he's into…"

"*She's* actually got quite the sense of humour." Ben walks over to me. "So what did you want to talk about? I'm on my break now, so I've got plenty of time."

I take a deep breath. "Ben, I have to leave."

"What?"

"I have to go, leave Orvale. See, I remembered something from before I came here, and I need to follow it up."

"What was it? Tell me." Ben's mood brightens somewhat.

"I, um…" I think about how to phrase it. "It's a bit personal, I don't--"

"Come *on*, you can tell me."

"…I remember my dad abusing me. And my mum stepping in to comfort me, but then he threatened her, and I had a friend who sort of took care of me when I got hurt. But I have to go and try to find out what happened."

His expression changes to one of pity, and he's silent for a couple of moments, before he replies. "If you have to go, then let me go with you."

# CHAPTER VI

I've known Aidan for a year, and I've always known him to be a nice, considerate person, who's just kind for the sake of being kind. Hell, I found him when he washed up on the beach last year, I helped him when he was so vulnerable, and that's just what you'd do if anyone was in that situation, but he felt as if he had to make it all up to me.

It was actually a pretty calm evening that day, I'd just finished work and I was walking along the beach cause I'd been stressed all through my shift. I remember watching the sunset and feeling great, it's the sort of thing you can just look at and feel better. It's a ritual for me; if I'm upset after a day of work then I'll walk to the beach and watch the sun go down.

It's funny, I actually remember listening to a song when I walked down. That song now gives me chills, because it makes me imagine my friend being so damn scared, and me being unable to help him. Even the lyrics are haunting. *Now I lay me down to sleep, pray the Lord my soul to keep.*

I saw a figure in the distance, lying on the sand. As I walked closer, I saw that it was a boy with dark brown hair, dressed in a zipped cream hoodie and dark jeans, both of which were soaked. He actually looked peaceful, as if he was asleep rather than unconscious.

*And if I die before I wake, pray the Lord my soul to take.*

I ran over to him, trying to wake him up. "What happened? Are you okay?"

He stirred, turned over and opened his eyes. They were quite childlike, full of light, undecided to be green or blue. I still can't decide which they are, not even when I see him every day.

"Where am I?"

"You're on the beach. What happened to you, man?"

"I don't remember." His voice came out in a stutter.

"You don't remember anything? Not even your name?"

"Aidan."

"Sorry?"

"That's my name. Aidan. But I don't remember

anything else, I don't know who you are, or where I am."

"Well I'm Ben. It's good to meet you, man. Are you sure you're okay?"

"I should be. I think as long as I can orientate myself, something should help me remember. I'm guessing you don't know me then?"

"No. I've never seen you around here before. And it looks like the tide carried you here rather than you just walking here and passing out, so God only knows where you came from."

Thinking about it now, I remember Aidan flinching a bit at the sound of 'God'.

"Okay. Okay, well I'll probably stay in town for a few days to get my bearings so do you know anywhere I can go, a youth shelter or something?"

"There isn't anything like that here, but you can stay with me."

"No." he said instantly. "I couldn't do that. You've only just met me, I wouldn't want to impose on you."

"Please. Aidan, you've washed up on a beach with nothing but the clothes you're wearing. Let me help you."

I saw him fishing around in his pockets for anything, but he came up short. "Fine." He sighed.

"But only until I find my feet. No longer."

Aidan stayed with me for two days before he got a job, but my mum helped him find a little cottage and enroll him at school. He got his first wage slip and said he'd pay her back, but she refused and told him to buy himself something. He used it to get a weekly shop in, and the rest is history. He's scraped by for a year, and is looking to be in good nick.

So when he comes into the shop to tell me that a memory has surfaced, I'm gobsmacked. "What was it? Tell me."

"I, um…" He hesitates. "It's a bit personal, I don't—"

I have the urge to just tell him that I don't care about how personal it is, that anything is something, but I just push gently. "Come *on*, you can tell me."

"…I remember my dad abusing me." *What?* "And my mum stepping in to comfort me, but then he threatened her, and I had a friend who sort of took care of me when I got hurt. But I have to go and find out what happened."

It takes me a few minutes to work out what he's said. So his dad was abusive, most likely alcoholic, and hit Aidan and probably his mum as well. He had a best friend who cared about him, who helped him out when he got hurt, who knew what was going on, sort

76

of like me. And he needs to leave to find out who they were or are.

I think about where he could be going, and if he goes alone then I don't know where he might end up. I decide to take a risk.

"If you have to go, then let me go with you."

"No." Someone else enters, a guy our age with silvery platinum-blond hair and shining green eyes.

"You can't come. It has to just be the two of us." His voice is sharp and I almost feel threatened.

"Who are you, then?"

Aidan interjects. "Ben, this is Noah. He's come here recently and he told me that he knew me from before I lost my memory. He sort of brought on the flashbacks I've been having--"

"Wait, flashbacks? What do you mean? You never told me." I'm a bit agitated now. He's been having memories come back and he's been keeping them from me?

"Well they started on Friday when I fainted in class. That was when I had the first memory, and then they've just come on a night; when I've fallen asleep my subconscious memories have come back as dreams." he explains.

"Okay, that's not that bad. But still, you should have told me, man. Let me go with you."

"No. You can't come with us." Noah says. I can

tell that he's getting assertive, and Aidan stiffens next to him.

"Hey, I'm just trying to help my friend here, I don't know who you are but I think I know what's better for him than you do."

"How dare you say that, I knew him before he even came here, he used to be my best friend!"

"Noah." Aidan says sharply, dropping a hand on his shoulder to restrain him.

"Some friend you are, if you've only bothered to come looking for him now!" I snap, and Aidan glares at me.

"Ben, stop it. Noah, please don't get angry." Aidan tells us. "Honestly, if you want to come then I see no reason why you can't. But at some point you'll have to go back. If something really personal comes up and it offends you, or if you're put in harm's way, then I wouldn't be able to forgive myself. So I think that the only compromise is to let you come, but only so far." He looks at Noah, and back at me. "Is that reasonable?"

"I guess so. Only if you keep him in check though." I jerk my thumb at Noah, who flares up.

"I'm only doing this as a favour to Aidan. Make no mistake, if you get on my nerves I won't hesitate to hurt you." He points a finger straight at me, almost jabbing me in the chest with it.

"Behave, both of you. If you start something, wherever we go, then *I* won't hesitate to step in. Otherwise you'll just rip each other apart and I'll have to pick up the pieces, like I always do when my friends fight." he says bitterly. "Noah, you say you're doing this for me, then please just get along. Ben as well, it'll only be for a few days hopefully."

"That it will. We'll have to catch the plane tomorrow and then go by foot for a day after that, and maybe we'll reach our destination by the next day. At which time, we'll have to go on ourselves." Noah informs us calmly.

"Plane?" Both Aidan and I speak in unison.

"Yep. We have to go to the heart of...this." He hesitates slightly, as if he's trying to rephrase things. "Where it all started."

"Which is?"

"Aidan, you have relatives who are involved in Christianity, and they're rooted in the heart of the faith. So we have to go to where all that began."

"Bethlehem?" I guess.

Noah shakes his head and is about to answer, when Aidan takes the words right out of his mouth. "Rome."

# CHAPTER VII

We leave the shop, and instantly I'm filled with an unusual feeling. I can't decide, is it rage? Jealousy, even? How I acted when I spoke to Ben scares me.

"What happened in there?" Aidan asks me when we go to the supermarket for him to buy ingredients for our lunch.

"I don't know. I just…lost it. I snapped at him, and that's not like me." I say guiltily.

"I'm going to be honest, it shocked me. Seeing you get angry with someone, and with Ben no less. He's my friend, as are you, and if he is going to come with us, which knowing him he won't back down, then you two need to sort it out between you." He grabs a loaf of crusty bread and some cured meat. "As I said back there, I don't want to have to keep you from each other's throats."

I look down at the floor. "I want to get along with

him, cause he seems nice, but he was just so…ignorant."

"No he wasn't. It's not common knowledge that you and I knew each other beforehand, and I don't really know just how much I can trust you yet. Whether you and I were friends back then, I don't know and I'm not sure." he says sharply.

This makes me shrink away slightly. Aidan reproaching me was surprising; I almost expected him to come to my defence, whereas he revoked both Ben and me when we argued.

I think about exactly how I felt when I was there with Ben, and I start to worry. I acted completely out of character, differently to how I would act in Heaven. Maybe it's me being here? It certainly wasn't virtuous, me losing my patience. Nor was it acting in the most loving way, as I told Aidan. What's wrong with me?! Maybe I'm being…infected by sin? Or viciousness, even?

Well, maybe not being *infected*. That's a very negative way of looking at it. Coming closer to humanity, that's better. Because sin was the reason that Adam and Eve were cast from Eden, and it resides in all of us. And we are exposed to it daily, hence I must have seen, performed or otherwise taken part in an act of sin in my short few days here.

But nobody said that sinning was a bad thing. Adam

and Eve were set free from perfection when they
sinned, and if we don't know badness, then how can
we truly know goodness? They ate from the Tree of
Knowledge of Good and Evil, and so yes, they know
about the horrors of the world, but they also know of
the beauty and goodness of the world as well!
Practically every action is in some part a sin. Thoughts,
too. We think and theorise of possible situations and
feelings which involve sin and the act of sinning,
therefore aren't we all subject to sin, even Yahweh? Or
Asherah?

But if they were, then neither of them would be
perfect beings, because they're subject to sin. And if
they're not perfect, then does that mean neither am I?
Or Aidan?

My fingers curl, bunching up my shirt in
frustration. I'm desperately searching for some
reasoning, some explanation as to why this is
happening and why I'm being vicious.

"Earth to Noah, do you read me?"

"What?" I'm getting so wound up that I don't
notice Aidan standing right in front of me.

"Are you okay? Ever since we left the shop you've
been acting weirdly." he points out, taking a tin of
chopped tomatoes off the shelf.

"Yeah. I'm fine, don't worry." I say quickly. Too
quickly.

"If you say so." he says, but I can tell that he sees right through me. He can tell something's wrong. "You know that you can tell me whatever you need to tell me, yeah?"

"Yeah." I repeat, again a bit fast.

He nods slightly, turning and going back to his shopping and I follow him, head low.

We return home and Aidan makes us grilled sandwiches of prosciutto and mozzarella cheese, and we eat them on the beach, sitting down on the rocks and watching the waves.

The saltiness of the meat and the creamy, stringy texture of the mozzarella blend perfectly, and whilst they don't completely calm me down, they do a pretty good job. Just being with Aidan calms my spirit. He may not be the exact same one I knew, due to his amnesia, but he's definitely close enough.

The waves roll in, some breaking early and others waiting until they're almost upon the sand to break, spreading the water up to our ankles which dangle down from the rocks. It's weird, just how different things are here compared to...up there.

Granted, the two realms are very similar, but up there it's as if there is no sun. Yahweh makes the light, commands when it is and is not, and there's no particular way from which the light comes, no fixed point that rises and sets over a certain time period. It just does. But He abides by His own rules that He sets out, two of which are that there must be an equal amount of light and darkness and that through which only He can shine and create light. And the actual look and geography of the place is very different, it's all flat. And I mean *flat*, there are no hills or craters or anything, it's just solid, constant surface. Which in itself has the texture of a carpet, of clouds, but at the same time is extremely stable. So one could take anything, no matter how heavy, drop it on the 'ground', and there would be no change whatsoever. Only He can bring about change. Or rather, only He chooses to bring about change. I reckon Asherah could if She wanted to, She just hasn't wanted to.

Or She's scared of what will happen if She does.

We're all scared of Him. I remember hearing a phrase since I've come here, 'God is a comedian playing to an audience that is too afraid to laugh'. What I think it means is that He is so powerful, so strong, so knowing, that nobody dares say anything, let alone what they think He wants to hear, because what we think He wants to hear may not be what He actually does want to hear, if that makes sense? Humans can't know or understand Him, and so some will be too afraid to act, because if they act wrongly then He will take action against them. And even if they don't act wrongly, if they just don't act right then He could take action out of spite. He's like a dictator; nobody will speak out against what He says because they know, or worse don't know, what will happen if they do.

But when Aidan was cast out, Yahweh made an example out of him. He said that if anyone else questioned His authority or His power, then they would regret what they said. And when I was still up there, He would lock Himself away in His chambers, only to emerge to destroy something in the mortal realm.

He's insecure, and it now falls to Asherah to pick up the slack. She has to try and take action against what She sees as unfair, and the Virtues can only do so much. So that's why we need Aidan back. To mend ties with Him, and hopefully revert things to what they used to be.

After we finish off the sandwiches, I brief Aidan on what he'll need to take with him when we fly to Rome. "You're gonna want enough for five days, along with some other stuff I've brought. Could you let Ben know that he'll need things for about three nights?"

"Sure."

"Cause he'll have to leave at some point, and it's gonna take about two days for us to get there and see everything."

"Okay." Aidan heads upstairs to grab a large suitcase, and I follow to make sure he packs the right things. I see him putting toiletries into a small bag and folding clothes. The way he puts his clothes in has me entranced for some reason. He folds the sleeves down onto the torso of the shirt before folding the bottom up and the top down to the middle, then carefully checks it for unnecessary creases before placing it in flat on the bottom of the case.

"Is there anything I can help you with?"

"If you could grab my trainers out of the bottom of the wardrobe that'd be great." he says, seemingly debating about whether to put his clothes underneath or on top of his shoes. I cross to the wardrobe and pull out a black pair of Chuck Taylors, passing them to him along with a black pair of plimsolls. A bright third pair of shoes catches my eye from the back of the wardrobe, and I take them out and inspect them. They're also Chuck Taylors, but they're tri-coloured. The colours merge, yellow to orange to red, and there is a nice marbling effect created by the way they blend. It's almost like watching a sunset.

Aidan stands up. "These as well?"

"Yeah, please. I was going to put them in, but I didn't know whether they'd be well received in Rome."

"Why wouldn't they be?" I ask.

"Cause they're so bright. Compared to the black trainers, they stick out like a sore thumb."

"They're nice. Really nice. I'm surprised you haven't worn them before now." I say, putting them in the case on top of the folded shirts and jeans. "That okay for you?"

"Sure. Thanks." He smiles at me, taking his phone charger and putting it in a smaller pocket in the case. He then takes his wallet and starts rifling through it looking for change. A look of realisation then comes over his face. "Oh crap, how are we gonna pay for things over there?"

"I have it covered." I take a wallet out of my pocket, opening it to show a large amount of €500 notes. Aidan's eyes are like dinner plates.

"Noah, what...how did you...?"

"Ehh, it's all part of the deal. Like this." I take out a single €500 note. Concentrating on the note and the mental image of a second note that I hold in my hand, I gently pull on the note's edge and a second note appears in my other hand, duplicating it. "And if I really want to show off, I can do this," I place my hand flat on top of the two notes, and bring it upwards. Note after note is conjured out of thin air below my hand, so that within the blink of an eye I have a small stack of notes, each one identical to the first.

I fan the notes out for Aidan, who stares at me, unsure of what to say. "Pick one." He takes a note in his shaking hand, examining it by the light of the room.

"There's no visible watermark, and it certainly looks genuine. Granted, I wouldn't know how to tell a real one from a fake one, but..." He looks at me incredulously. "What the Hell?"

"Heaven." I correct with a smile. "I learnt it from Thomas, one of the Virtuous Ones, whose Core is generosity. He's very generous with money, and occasionally he used to take you and me down here where he'd pay us into a musical or something like that. He'd need a way to get his money, and the most honest way was to be smart and to duplicate it."

"Smart? You mean sly?"

"No, I mean smart. He never used it to be extravagant, he would just be generous and take us out to forget about the bad things if Yahweh gave either of us a bad time." I look down as Thomas' fate comes back to me. "He's not so good at the moment though, Yahweh found out about his powers of duplication and took them away from him. He's sad, and even a bit cold to people. Not to me, but to some others."

Aidan puts a reassuring hand on my shoulder. "It's okay. We'll sort it all out." He pauses, then asks

**89**

me, "Did I have any powers? As the brave one?"

"Yep. Yours was unusual though, you took power from your feelings."

"What do you mean?"

"The more emotionally driven you were, the stronger you were. Like, if you were really, really happy then your powers would make flowers bloom wherever you walked. Your negative emotions were interesting, as awful as it sounds. Cause if you were sad, it rained, but if you cried, then it would snow. And if you cried hard…"

"It would snow hard." He finishes my sentence for me. "Did we ever have a blizzard?"

"Once." I hold up a single finger. "And that was the first day Yahweh got angry with you. But we never knew what would happen if you got angry. We had rain, we had snow, we had spontaneous flowers, but we never had anything else. You never had a reason to get angry. Come to think of it, it's almost as if you had power over the elements."

"Then why don't I have it here?" he asks.

"Because you're in the mortal realm. And you were cast down forcefully, whereas I came here voluntarily so I keep my powers. When we pass through to the immortal realm, then we'll notice a change." Another thing comes to me. "You also had another power."

"Yeah?"

"You could almost cast spells. You'd sort of slip into a trance, speak in a language we wouldn't understand, and you'd make things happen. Mostly it was just something to calm people down or regulate emotions, but I reckon if you set your mind to it you'd be able to do more...varied things."

"Oh, that's awesome! So I was like a sorcerer or something?"

"Yep, you were incredibly powerful, as we all were."

"Wow." He smiles broadly, awestruck, before continuing. "So we're going to Heaven from Rome?"

"Not exactly. We're going to Heaven from Purgatory, and to Purgatory from Rome."

He zips up his suitcase and sets it down at the bottom of the stairs. "Purgatory?"

"Yeah. We have to go there in order to get to Heaven." We sit down on the sofa. "And it'll be hard. But there you'll be able to use your abilities. Passing through in Rome will change you back to an angel, because it's what you were before. If we were to take Ben through the barrier, he either wouldn't survive the jump or be killed by what we'd find in Purgatory."

"Which is what?"

"Well, from what I gather from Asherah, in Purgatory you are purged of your impurity and in particular of the Seven Deadly Sins: pride, greed, lust, envy, gluttony, wrath and sloth."

"Yeah?"

"And that's the thing. Every one of those seven sins resides in Purgatory, to stop the departed from purging themselves of them."

"What do you mean, resides?"

"I mean the sins themselves, in physical form. To rid yourself of your pride, you must overcome Pride itself. This is what she told me when she sent me here and I knew I'd have to come back the long way."

Aidan's eyes go wide, as he takes in this information. "We essentially have to kill the Seven Deadly Sins?"

"Not necessarily. You say 'kill', but what we'll do is merely overcome them, resist their urges. And it'll be difficult, cause each sin is a part of us. But if it gets us up there," I point upwards, "then it'll be worth it."

He's again silent for a few minutes. Then: "Okay. Okay, I think I understand." Aidan looks over at the setting sun. "I'll be on with dinner."

"Allow me. Please." I stand up, going to the kitchen and taking several food items from the cupboards and fridge. As I open some chicken thighs, slicing them up into pieces, my mind again wanders to Aidan.

The honest truth is I admire the guy. To take on as

much as he has, working so many hours at his job as to be entirely self-supportive, and keeping up his school studies at the same time, even just going about his day as he does, being so happy all the time...it takes enormous amounts of energy. In a childish way, I sort of feel like he's showing me up! But then again, I have to keep reminding myself that he has the soul of an angel, and it seems the heart to match.

He tries to be as selfless as possible, always doing his best to please. I wonder how Asherah managed to allocate him a Virtue, as he seems to embody three; Bravery, Comfort and Peace. And they don't necessarily go hand-in-hand all the time. Relativity dictates that virtues can and will come into conflict with each other. But sometimes, the brave thing to do is to give someone comfort, because some aren't as approachable as others, and sometimes it takes courage to even ask someone if they're alright. And it shows just in the incident between me and Ben that he's a peaceful being. He hates seeing people angry, or fighting. I guess the weather we had in Heaven just goes to show how he is. We had rain, snow, and flowers, but no angry weather from him; one can only speculate...

When I finish preparing a meal of enchiladas for us, we eat rather quietly. The silence is only broken by me asking Aidan if he's let Ben know that we set off tomorrow.

"Yep, we're catching the noon flight to Rome and we need to be at the airport by ten to allow plenty of time to get through airport security, hence we need to leave here at nine, and be up at half-eight as a result." He then adds, "And I've told Ben all of that."

I nod, impressed. I shouldn't be; he's always been sharp.

"And you've set us an alarm?"

"I have that." He nods, and I smile at his efficiency. "The only thing left to do is get a good night's sleep tonight and go through with things tomorrow."

After we've eaten, we both wash the dishes and head upstairs. It's decided that I can share a bed with Aidan, but I don't want to impose on him so we're quite distinct in how we sleep. In other words, if so much as one finger crosses the middle of the bed I'm pretty sure I'll see what happens when he gets angry. Obviously, we both sleep in nightclothes, and it's not as bad as I thought. He's not awkward about our sleeping arrangements, which is good, but I'm still surprised when his arms wrap around me in the night, and he gently holds me close. I feel safe. I yet again wonder what his Core really is. He may not be merely Brave. There is a rumour amongst the Virtuous Ones that says that when Asherah was creating us, she assigned a couple of us more than one Virtue. Maybe he's one of them?

Thinking about it, this wouldn't surprise me. Aidan's special, in more ways than one. He's different to the rest of us, but then again we're all different to each other. But if he's one, then who's the other? And what Virtues would they embody? I think that if Aidan was one, then he'd be brave, peaceful and quite kind. So the other would need to complement him, by being tolerant, sort of different maybe? So that Aidan could balance out the difference by making people react well? It's hard to find virtues that don't necessarily work together, cause they all have some link to each other.

Anyway, now's not the time to be thinking about this. I have plenty of time on the flight tomorrow for that...

I drift off to sleep, resting my head on Aidan's chest, and I swear I hear him utter a soft sigh of relief.

# CHAPTER VIII

*Eyes on the hourglass, as we sink into the sand, time's up, there's nothing we can do about it, it's fine, love, cause I know I'mma live without it...*

I hear a woman's singing voice, and I know it as Aidan's alarm. He reaches over to switch it off, urging me to get up. We both change into our normal clothes, and Aidan takes two Panini out of the fridge for us when we get downstairs. Throwing one over to me, he unwraps the cling film from his own and takes a large bite. I realise that he's made us chicken and bacon sandwiches, with mayonnaise; I eat mine with relish, savouring the mix of flavours and trying once again to distract myself from what we're about to do.

Three of us—well, two of us really—are travelling across Europe to find the entrance to Purgatory. From there we hope to ascend to Heaven. Yahweh help...wait, maybe he's not the best example. Asherah help us. That's better.

I take a look outside and see that Ben's standing by the road. I grab our suitcases and take them out while Aidan locks up. "Hey."

"Hey. How you doing?"

"Alright, thanks. You?"

"Yeah, I'm okay. More worried about how I'm gonna pay for this though…"

"Ben, don't worry. Tell you what, I'll send you the money over when we're at the airport."

"What? Noah, I couldn't let you do that."

"I insist. It's my way of apologising for snapping at you yesterday. I shouldn't have been so nasty."

"I should apologise. It was my fault."

"No, it wasn't. Plus, I'm sending the money over whether you like it or not, so if you don't want the money then at least spend it on this one." I nod discreetly at Aidan. "Neither of you know how lucky you are to have each other's backs. You're both awesome people."

"Wow. Thanks, man." He looks at me with a mixture of reverence and surprise, then disregards it when Aidan joins us. "Are we ready then?"

"Aye." He nods, and I take my suitcase as we walk down to the train station.

After we manage to get through the airport security, we walk up the steps to get on the plane that is set to depart at midday. I'm really excited, we're actually going! Things are moving forwards!

The three of us take our seats near the back of the plane, and Ben sits by the window intending to sleep, allowing Aidan and I to talk. The plane takes off and the g-force hits, pulling me back into the seat. Aidan takes out a pillow from his hand luggage and lays it across both of our headrests. "Well, you've got what you wanted, man." he manages to say over the roar of the engines.

"Yep. And I'm thanking both of them that you agreed in the end."

"Ehh, it's no problem. Plus, if my 'angel powers'," he makes air quotes, "are anything like you say, then when we come back I'll be able to get my own back on whoever pisses me off." Aidan adds with a somewhat dark laugh.

"I think you'll be able to use them here, I can so I don't see why you shouldn't. I'm more hoping that Tom and the others will recognise you; they were devastated when you left."

"I shouldn't be so different, I mean what's changed, really? Apart from my opinion of Yahweh?"

"I guess you're right." I take a calming breath, leaning back against the pillow. I close my eyes softly, and Aidan's voice comes to me in my mid-slumber.

"So was it only the Virtuous Ones, Yahweh, and

Asherah in Heaven, then?"

"No. There were others. We had centurions."

"Wait, those are soldiers, yeah?"

"That's right. We had soldiers in case anything happened in the Inferno that we needed clearing up, or if any unsavoury characters happened to slip through Purgatory by accident. I remember one case where I was on gate duty, and this Ukrainian guy came up the steps. He started shouting at me, I didn't understand but it all sounded really offensive. Then you actually came over and translated for him. You had the gift of glossolalia, and--"

"Gift of *what*?"

"Glossolalia. Speaking in tongues. It's part of your embodying Peace, you can unite people through language. You said something to him, and he snapped right back at you. Then one of the centurions took him by the wrist and sent him back to the bottom of Purgatory. They can warp wherever they want, and so it's incredibly difficult to take one of them on, let alone a fleet of them."

"It sounds it. But that glass-whatever doesn't sound like me."

"*Glossolalia*. And it *was* you. You knew in your mind exactly what these people were saying. And you told me that you heard both the man's voice and your own voice as English, but to everyone else it was another language. The rest of us heard you talking in Ukrainian. It was terrifying to watch though, because I just heard the guy sounding angry, and you replied as calmly as you could, then he bit your head off."

"My teachers did tell me that I was good at languages. I took German at school when I first came, then I couldn't do it this year because of subjects, but I've never lost that knowledge."

"That proves it. You have an affinity for language. Granted, some are harder than others to learn, like Japanese and Chinese, with being different scripts and very nasal languages, but otherwise you should be able to pick one up with ease."

A large smile spreads across Aidan's face. "Wow. I'm trying to take this all with a pinch of salt --and a pretty big one at that-- but it's amazing to even imagine. That I could do all that."

"It's astounding. If anyone in the mortal realm got their hands on us in our pure Forms, then we'd be paraded as the next step in genetics. But ultimately it would reveal the existence of Heaven, the Inferno and everything. It would plunge us into turmoil."

"I know."

"Which is why I only duplicated the money, or used any of my powers, within the privacy of your house."

"What else can you do?"

101

"Well I'm the Form of the Comfort, so I can regulate the immediate temperature to make someone feel just alright. Not too warm, nor too cold. When we shared a bed, I lowered the temperature slightly to stop either of us from overheating.

"But apart from that, I'm quite like you. I can help keep emotions in check. I have an infectious aura, which spreads to others. My being there with someone else will help calm them, comfort them."

"So both of our powers are quite passive?"

"I suppose you could put it like that. Just small things. You and I, we can't massively affect people, I don't think. I've never tried to focus my energy, and I wonder what would happen if I did…"

Thinking about it, I reckon that the best I could hope for would be if I could transform my aura into a physical form, a staff or symbol, something like that. It'd certainly be interesting if I could, as if our…altercation, for want of a better word, with Yahweh turns into anything other than just a debate, then we'll need something to fight Him with. And I don't want to rely on my aura alone.

The thing with Yahweh is, He never forgives. He condemned Lucifer to the Inferno until the end of time, and He never gave Aidan a second positive thought, only ever associating him with rebellion. So that shows, I guess, how cruel He is in reality. But we don't have to look that far to see how He really is.

If we look at nature, there are plenty of horrible beings that exist. Animals and plants that kill other animals and plants in awful ways, like pitcher plants that dissolve the bodies of flies and frogs in acid. Digger wasps who lay their eggs inside a live cockroach, then the eggs hatch and larvae eat the cockroach from the inside out. It's terrifying, just how cruel nature is. But then if nature is cruel, then that by extension means that the being who created nature to be cruel, is in themselves cruel. Hence Yahweh, because He is responsible for these things, is immoral. But He's one side of the story, whereas Asherah is responsible for the better things. They operate in a dualistic system, with good and bad, positive and negative, being equal in creation and manifestation. In other words, Asherah is positive, but She can have Her 'off days', whereas Yahweh has become negative, with just a flicker of goodness. They complement each other, but because the balance has gone out of whack, we need a miracle.

We need Aidan.

As we descend, and Aidan briefly goes to the aeroplane toilet, I wake Ben up. "We're landing."

"Hmm? Oh, okay." he says groggily.

"Ben, just to let you know, when we get to Rome we'll stay for a few days, go to the Vatican City, but then you'll have to leave."

"Oh, I know. Aidan told me."

"And you're okay with that, yeah?"

"Of course. I knew that there'd be a point when I'd have to leave to let you two go on your own, so it wasn't that much of a surprise."

Thank Asherah. "That's good. We'll try and fit as much in, in these few days as we can though, so that this wasn't a complete waste for you."

"Noah, it would never have been a waste. I've always wanted to see the world. And seeing Rome and the Vatican now, it's all good."

I breathe a sigh of relief. "Thank you for being so understanding."

"It's no problem, man."

Aidan comes back, and sits down next to me. "So where to first, boss?"

"We're booked in at a hotel near the Pantheon, so it shouldn't be hard to find. We can just get a taxi there from the airport." I say, getting my wallet ready.

We step off the aeroplane, but as soon as his feet touch the ground, Aidan lets out a pained shout and grabs my wrist in panic.

# CHAPTER IX

As soon as I step off the plane, a huge burst of pain in my head threatens to knock me out.

I clamp my hands to my head, and as I look around me, I see visions flash before my eyes. People walking on clouds, an immensely large, powerful man, and a woman whose very essence calms my soul. The pain stops, and the visions are all that I see. I see a very familiar silver-haired young man, who approaches me.

"Come on, Tom's gonna take us both out tonight! We can forget about what happened earlier…" he says to me, and I'm relieved.

"Thank the Lady, that was terrifying, what He did…"

"I know. But you're safe now. And at least we know for next time." He touches my arm gently, and now I'm on the ground, with the larger man almost stomping on my chest and pushing me into the earth. I'm falling, down through the air, and all I see is black.

And then it hits me.

*Oh no. It's all true.*

I *was* an angel, living in Heaven. And Yahweh cast me down, and Asherah defended me, and Noah was by my side. They were my family, and they loved me.

I'm torn up suddenly. I don't know whether to feel happy cause Noah was right, or relieved cause I've got my memories back, or amazed cause I was an immortal being.

But instead, I'm filled with rage.

Yahweh hurt me. He upset Noah. He moved Asherah to sorrow. He causes destruction and pain to mortals with the things He does, and the sheer volume of people who have died as a result of His misinterpreted instructions is heart-breaking.

He needs to pay. He must learn that His creations have feelings, no matter how far beneath Him they are. He brought the destruction upon Himself, in allowing Adam and Eve to be tempted by the Serpent in Eden. He knew that they wouldn't be able to resist, and yet He created them so anyway. If I didn't know any better, I'd have thought that Yahweh planned for them to be led astray by the Serpent, to bring the corruption of Original Sin upon their lineage.

But I can't let it show.

I can't. Noah would never look at me the same

way. He'd hate me for my intentional rebellious streak. He pitied me for making the mistake once, if I make it twice then it's worthy of shame.

"Aidan! Are you okay?"

Noah's voice snaps me back to reality.

"Yeah. I'm fine. Just a head rush, that's all. A drop in blood pressure from standing up too fast." I laugh it off, and a look of relief crosses his face.

"That's good. I thought you were hurt." The three of us leave the plane and head into the airport to get our luggage. Ben casts me a glance, and mouths to me. *Blood pressure?*

I nod to him, and he nods back. *Okay.*

As we take our suitcases and Noah hails a taxi, I start to worry about his perceptions and what he thinks of what happened. *He could know… He could be perfectly aware of your recall, and he could have known it would happen all along. Maybe he intended it. Maybe he wanted you to see it, so you'd believe him, or tap into everything you once had as an angel?*

*No. Stop.* I tell myself. *Maybe he did intend it, but whatever he did or didn't intend, you need to tell him at some point. You're sharing a room in the hotel, so tell him then!*

I'll let him know later, or tomorrow. Or in a few days, when Ben's gone. Then we can discuss it properly. Yeah. That sounds good.

We get into the taxi, taking up three of the six seats in the back. As Noah and Ben converse lightly, and I look out of the window over the Roman cityscape, I contemplate just how the entrance to Purgatory is located in the Vatican. Sure, St Peter's Basilica is a huge landmark, and the view from the top of the spire is glorious, but I don't see how we can go to Purgatory... Maybe there's some kind of rift in the fabric of the Universe, or some other conspiracy theory material like that? I smile to myself at the ludicrousness of it all, but then quickly realise that it must exist, as my memories state.

I remember the other Virtuous Ones as well! Thomas, Phoebe, Nathaniel, Seth, I remember a particular girl called Lily whom Yahweh seemed to be rather harsh towards... I wonder why. And of course, Noah himself, exactly the same in the visions as now. He was always so kind, so calming. He really embodied Comfort, lifting us up if we were upset. And

I remember having...feelings for him? Well, friendship. We were best friends up there, and it's easy to see why. He's welcoming, kind, he's a rare sort of person who's incredibly altruistic. He and I both feel that we must act in the kindest way, which isn't always necessarily the best way...it's got me in trouble more than once, being nice over acting correctly.

But for once, I feel like I belong. Granted, I

belong when I'm in Orvale, but at the same time I could easily belong in Heaven. A choice between my old friends and my new ones, it's difficult! But I'll cross that bridge when I come to it. Right now, I need to focus on what's to come.

I see that we're coming into the city, off the motorway, and we pull up outside a hotel. Noah pays and thanks the driver, we get out of the taxi, and as I hear the receptionist speaking, she speaks to me in English. "Good afternoon sirs, may I help you?"

"Yes please, we have a reservation?"

"Under what name, sir?"

I turn to Noah. "What name did you have us under?"

He looks bewildered. "Umm, Smith I think…"

"Thanks." I turn back to the woman. "We're under the name of Smith, we should be on the third floor?"

She looks down a sheet of paper with neat writing. "Okay, there you are, Mr Smith, and here's your key." She takes one off a hook behind her and hands it to me. "Have a lovely stay here, sirs, and we'll look forward to greeting you for breakfast in the morning."

"Thank you, miss."

"It's my pleasure." She smiles at me, and I head for the elevator, Ben and Noah in tow.

**109**

When we pull our suitcases in, Noah asks me, "What in Lucifer's name was that?"

"What was what?"

"That! Back there!" he says, exasperatedly pointing in the direction of the reception desk.

"Dude, you just spoke fluent Italian to her!" Ben tells me, and I'm confused.

"No I didn't, I spoke English! Or that's what it sounded like…"

Noah grasps my wrist in an iron grip, and speaks to me in a low voice so Ben can't hear. "What?!"

"It sounded like English, what she was saying to me."

Noah's sensitivity makes me think. Why would he react so harshly? Unless my powers as an angel have come back as a result of being in the vicinity of Purgatory? Or at least my glossolalia.

"Is everything okay?"

"Yeah. Yeah, everything's fine Ben, don't worry." Noah says to him calmly. The elevator dings, and we step out, walking across the hall. I take out my key and unlock the door.

The room's not that bad, quite spacious, with space for our suitcases and an en-suite for us to freshen up. I start to unpack, and Ben tells me that he's going to take a shower. As soon as the bathroom door locks, Noah sits down on my bed.

"Spill. What happened?"

"I told you, I heard her speaking English."

"But we heard you speaking Italian as if it was your mother tongue. And after what I told you on the plane…" His voice trails off, and I straighten up to look him in the eye.

"What are you implying?"

"I think your powers have come back. Or something like that."

I then decide that there's no point in pretending any more. "Why did Yahweh hate Lily?"

"What?"

"There was a girl called Lily among the Virtuous ones. Why did Yahweh dislike her?"

"She reminds him of the first woman."

"You mean Eve?"

"I mean Lilith. She was Adam's first wife, not Eve. 'In his image he created them, male and female he created them.' That female was Lilith, who then abandoned Adam after she refused to be subservient to him. She fled Eden, and Yahweh made Adam another wife from his own being."

"From his rib."

"Yep. And because Lily reminded Yahweh of Lilith, he had a distaste for her that he could never explain." Noah pauses to think. "So you remember everything?"

"Yeah. I remember the other angels, I remember Tom taking us out after Yahweh had got angry with me the first time, I remember you being my best friend. You were always there for me, Noah."

"Phoebe asked me once how you and I got along so well. I told her that we just clicked." He gives me a half-smile.

"Maybe. Maybe we were meant to stop Yahweh, and that's why we get along, cause we need to synergise."

"Possibly. Well seeing as the glossolalia you demonstrated downstairs has come back, I guess your other powers may come back in time." Noah resumes his unpacking, as do I, and Ben emerges from the bathroom just as I take out a canister of deodorant; I toss it to him on instinct and he sprays himself.

"Thanks, man. I swear you know me just as well as I know myself."

"No problem. So," I turn to face Noah, "where to first?"

"Well it's late now, but I think we can afford to just do some general sightseeing tomorrow, maybe we'll find something around that'll give us a lead on your past."

Of course. We're still unaware of any real evidence, as far as Ben knows.

"Okay. Well the Pantheon could help? It's one of

**112**

the most widely recognised things in Rome, so if I'd seen anything in the past that would be it."

"I'll check the train timetables for tomorrow morning, and we can catch the underground. Fair warning though, the Roman trains are...shaky, to put it mildly."


Shaky is an understatement.

After we have dinner downstairs in the hotel, we get to sleep quite quickly, and board the trains the next morning. The subway system is fast-paced in Rome, and we set off with a start; Ben is thrown into a tall lady with large blonde hair, Noah grabs onto me for support and I crash into the side of the train. As Ben apologises in broken Italian that he learnt from a phrase book on the way here, I take hold of a safety rail and pull myself up, Noah with me. I can tell that I'm blushing, and Noah cracks a smile.

"You alright?"

"Bit battered, but the train will be okay." I smirk, and I take a quick look around me. There are people literally everywhere, the carriage is cramped enough to be able to dismiss two guys who are squished together. My back is flush against the glass of the doors, and one arm is casually around Noah so I can grip the railing and ensure that we're not separated.

**113**

Ben negotiates his way to us. "What are you guys expecting when you get there?"

"I reckon more than anything, some kind of recall. Repressed memories will often cause chains of other memories to be revealed when familiar surroundings are near. In other words, I should see something when we reach the Parthenon."

"Okay, as long as you know what you're looking for. Cause I wouldn't have the faintest clue to be honest." He gives a small laugh, but I can see something in his eyes. Maybe disbelief?

I try to forget it, but it's still bugging me when we step off the train. What if Ben doesn't think I'm getting these memories as we go, what if he realises I'm faking it, but not in the way he thinks? If he does cotton on, then I need a backup. I can't just tell him the complete truth; he'd never believe me. Noah and I need to properly talk about this, about what the foil is should Ben see through me.

We reach the Pantheon, but when we enter and see statues of Zeus and Hera, as well as the other Olympians, Noah desperately looks to me as a stab of pain between my eyes subjects me to another vision.

# CHAPTER X

We enter the Pantheon, with its marble floor and huge stone pillars, and I'm on edge. I realise that the portrayal of the Olympians could trigger another memory recall, and I keep my eyes on Aidan. He looks around at the statues, and back at me. He then falls to the floor, clutching his head in pain and opening his eyes wide.

"Aidan, stay with me. Please."

He has my hand in an iron grip, and I flinch at how strong his grasp is. He suddenly relaxes, regaining his composure and taking a calming breath. I stand up, and the brunette does so as well, casting a glance around himself at the statues of Athena, Hera, Artemis, Aphrodite, Demeter and Hestia. "They're all like Her. Like Asherah. Wisdom, marriage, the moon, beauty, nature and the home." He then looks across to Apollo. "Whereas only Apollo isn't like Yahweh. Hephaestus, Poseidon, Hades, Ares and Zeus play large roles in Olympus. Apollo is merely a messenger. But the other gods cause destruction. Fire, the seas, the

Underworld, war and thunder, they're all reminders of suffering. Apollo was the god of the sun, poetry, music and art. All good things."

"He was also the god of plague. Which wasn't exactly good." I contest, but I realise that I'm digressing. "What did you see?"

"I saw Them. Yahweh and Asherah. They changed into the Olympians, each splitting up into individual deities, and Yahweh's whole attire changed; a white toga for Zeus, water cloaking his body for Poseidon, gold and red armour for Hephaestus, battle armour for Ares and a robe as black as night for Hades.

"Asherah changed as well. Hera held a staff in her hand and wore a floor-length white dress with the sleeves wrapping round her shoulders, Athena wore battle armour, Artemis had a quiver on her back and a cut-off dress, Hestia just had a simple white robe and a laurel wreath, Demeter had on a lace dress that looked like vines trailing over her, and Aphrodite went all out with a purple and gold oriental dress, bangles, anklets, and flowers braided through her hair that stretched down her back.

"Then they all reformed into the one goddess. Asherah Herself created huge daises with purple and silver sashes and drops, like a wedding. She made a moon which shone down upon the earth, flowers which sprouted and bloomed, and gorgeous maidens dressed in white appeared with gifts. Dresses, a coronet and a shield."

"The aegis." I gesture to the Athena statue. She's holding a shield with the head of Medusa on it. "It's the symbol of the goddess, she would fight using it."

"But Yahweh intervened. The five gods destroyed the moon that Asherah had created with lightning, burned up the fabrics with fire, killed the maidens with battle weapons, made the plants perish in huge torrents of water, and then just plunged it all into darkness."

"It sounds like what we have to do. Yahweh will try and kill us. We have to defend ourselves and overcome Him. And if that means getting the other Virtuous on our side, that's what we have to do."

"Okay. But if this is what I see when I come in here, then I don't want to think about my vision in the Vatican."

I take his hand in mine and squeeze it reassuringly. "You'll be okay. I'm your guardian, aren't I? I'm here to help you. And when the time comes, to fight alongside you."

I look at Aidan. His eyes are bright with a determination I've never seen before. His expression tells me that he's safe in the knowledge that he doesn't have to worry, that I'll be by his side until the end, that everything will be alright.

"Someone care to tell me what the hell you two have been smoking?"

I flinch, and turn to see Ben standing right in front of us.

"Yeah, I'm still here." he says bitterly. "I heard every fucking word of that. Now tell me what's going on. And don't even think to spare my feelings, I honestly couldn't care less about what you have to say. I just want to hear it from you, Aidan, and not this tosser." He jerks his thumb at me threateningly.

I try to start well, cutting between Aidan and Ben. "Ben, listen--"

*"NO! YOU FUCKING LISTEN TO ME!"* he roars. "I've come all the way here, thinking that I'm helping Aidan out, and then he goes and has some kind of drug-induced fit? He starts seeing things, you're spouting off about guardians, and I'm meant to just take this in my stride, all this crap that I've never even heard of before now? Tell me the truth." he demands. "Who. Are. You."

I squirm. "I could tell you, but you wouldn't believe me."

"After what I just saw, after my best friend faints before my eyes and then there you are, I'm in the mood for any explanation. That or just a reason to batter you."

Aidan takes a calming breath. "Why don't we take this outside, rather than causing a scene here?"

"Fine." He acquiesces, and we leave the building.

Finding a secluded spot, I confess everything to Ben. About how Aidan and I are both angels, about how Yahweh cast Aidan down after he questioned Yahweh's power, about how I've been sent by Asherah to bring him back, and about how the portal to the immortal realm is in the Vatican.

Aidan then fills in the gaps about the Pantheon. "So when I got in there, I just had a vision of Yahweh and Asherah changing into the Olympians. It freaked me out, and Noah had to console me."

Ben is silent, his face unchanging like the marble on the Pantheon floor. "Okay. Okay, so you washed up in Orvale because God cast you out of Heaven?"

"Yes."

"And you're here," he points at me, "to bring him back?"

"Yep." I say.

"And all this is to fix God's insecurity problems?"

"Pretty much." I'm just thankful he believes us.

But then—

"Bullshit. You're both crazy." he accuses. "Both of you! Especially *you*, Aidan!"

**119**

The brunette looks scared of Ben. Terrified, even, of someone he calls his best friend. And I can't take it anymore, the injustice of it all.

I lunge at Ben, pinning him to the wall. In a burst of anger, I start shouting. "You think you know *anything* about what he's been through? You think you have *any* right to believe or disbelieve what he says?!" I snarl, pressing my fingertips to his temples.

I channel my energy into him, pumping him full of my memories and showing him exactly what happened to Aidan. Ben's eyes open wide in fear, and I can see that he's watching the memories unfold before him. Aidan's Fall, my treatment at the hands of Yahweh, Asherah's request and my coming to Orvale.

"You want to see things? *Here*." I draw from Aidan's mind, and show the vision to Ben. In doing so, I see it in all its horror. Five huge gods bringing death and war upon Heaven, and I actually notice a sixth god in the background, someone whom Aidan must have been unaware of. He stands rather hunched over, as if he's afraid of the others. But his attire intrigues me; he's dressed in a pair of winged sandals, a robe like Artemis' in that it's a cut-off piece with a belt around the waist, with a quiver of arrows on his back and a beautifully carved bow in His hand. He's like her twin.

"*Apollo*." I breathe, realising that all six of the

gods are there, and the symbolism of it all. The goodness in Yahweh is trapped and overpowered by the malicious and negative emotions raging inside Him. Just so here, the five more powerful gods are destroying everything, and the goddesses and Apollo are powerless to stop them.

But where Aidan's must have ended, this vision continues. Apollo and Artemis run to each other and embrace, and Hera raises her staff. Athena grasps her aegis and as the twins spirit away the maidens' bodies, Aphrodite creates thousands of twittering birds to flock around Hephaestus, brutally pecking him to death. The marriage goddess destroys Zeus with a blast from her staff, as Athena's shield glows brightly and Poseidon dissolves into water vapour. Demeter creates enormous roots which attack Ares before throttling him. Hestia then emanates a huge burst of pink energy from her being, and Hades is forced to his knees; she approaches him, grabbing him by the neck, and blinds him by forcing daggers made of the same pink energy into his eyes.

With the five gods dead, the remaining five goddesses look at me, their dresses spattered with blood, and their expressions are grim. The vision ends, and I jump back from Ben with a start.

*Oh dear Lucifer... What did I do?* I'm shaking, and I grab onto the side of a building to ground myself.

Aidan is at Ben's side, with a hand on his shoulder.

"You saw my vision, didn't you?"

He's got sweat streaming down his face. "It was horrible, they... There was so much death... Oh my god, you've got to kill Him, haven't you?"

"We have to try."

Ben pulls Aidan into a hug. "I never believed either of you, and...it's all true."

"Ben, it's okay. There's nothing to apologise for. I saw exactly what you saw. All of that death, the viciousness of the goddesses... You're right, it *was* horrible. But Noah and I have to be strong and face Yahweh. That's why you need to go home before us. So that we can go up to Heaven and sort things out. We'll both come back though. There's no doubt about that."

He sniffs. "Okay. It's a lot to take in at once, though..."

"I know. It was hard for me as well. But I accept it, and I make do." Aidan sees me watching them, and he smiles. "We both do."

I'm moved by his commitment, and I don't know why, but I start crying. He lets go of Ben and hugs me.

"It's okay, Noah. Let it out, dude."

I'm disgusted by the way I've acted towards Ben. The fury I've felt towards him, it's disgraceful. And

I'm afraid of this anger, what if I show it towards Aidan? He doesn't deserve it! Neither of them do. And it's so unlike me to be angry, I'm not worthy of embodying Peace. Aidan should have got that instead, as well as being brave. He's everything I could wish to be, and he seems to handle things better than me.

"I'm so sorry, to both of you…"

"Why? What have you done wrong?"

"I've given in to my anger. I was so nasty to Ben, and I don't want to risk being that way with you."

"Noah. Look at me." I do. "You're only doing the best you can. You're being the only thing you can be, which is yourself. Don't apologise for getting angry, or falling short. That's what makes you human."

"But I'm not! I'm… We're both angels. Not humans."

"We've sinned. Nothing's wrong with that. As you said, sin set Adam and Eve free. And even anger is a virtue, in the form of exercising the right amount of anger. So you're being the best embodiment of your Virtue you can be. Nobody is more peaceful than you, because in order to know true peace, you must also know unrest. And you've experienced a moment of unrest now."

I wipe my eyes, and look up at him, smiling weakly. "Thanks, Aidan."

"It's okay. Forget the fact that you need to

protect me, I think sometimes it's me who has to tell you that it'll be alright."

"Yeah, s'pose so." I stand up, brushing the dust off my jeans.

Ben looks over at me. "I never thought you were being honest with me. Noah...I shouldn't have been so cruel to you. That's not like me. And it's unlike me to have such a... such an instant dislike of people. To not trust them. So for that, I apologise."

"It's okay. I didn't expect you to believe me, but when you didn't believe Aidan, even after what you saw in the Pantheon, I just snapped."

"Hey, at least I've seen the thing for myself. And it's helped me understand it a bit more."

Aidan himself interjects here. "And now that this is sorted, let's go get things in order. Noah, as much as I hate to say it, when do we need to pass through the barrier?"

"Chances are we'd be best doing it the day after next. So that we can stake out the Vatican tomorrow, and pass through the barrier the day after." I say.

"Alright. In that case, Ben, you'll need to catch a flight back on Thursday."

"Okay. Noah, you gave me the money before, right?" Ben asks me.

"Yep. You should be able to just get a seat there and then, otherwise I'll come along and help out."

"You're not gonna use some kind of Jedi mind trick on the airport staff, are you?"

"Damn, there goes my whole plan..." I laugh quickly, catching myself. Cursing... that ain't good. I'm definitely sinning.

Thankfully, Aidan doesn't seem to notice, as we make our way back into the plaza to grab some food.

When we get back to the hotel that evening, the three of us play cards to pass the time. "So what *did* happen when you got off the plane, Aidan?" Ben inquires.

"What do you mean?"

"I mean did you have a rush of blood pressure? Or was that a vision as well?"

"It was a vision. I'm sorry for lying to you, but I couldn't tell you then. You'd never have believed me. Plus, it was mainly for Noah to know." He glances at me.

"Also," I say, "what happened in the hotel earlier with Aidan speaking Italian, that's a reflection of his life in Heaven. He could communicate with anyone, no matter what language they spoke. But he never knew he was doing it, his mind translated it into English to him, when to us he was speaking another language. That's why he was so nonchalant earlier about it, right?"

"Yeah."

"Wow." Ben says. "That's pretty cool, if you ask me. So what else can you do? Or what could you do in Heaven?"

"Well my powers were tied to my emotions. So if I felt a strong emotion, it'd have an effect on the environment around me. Like, if I was really happy, then it'd make the earth around me sprout flowers. If I was sad, it'd rain. If I cried, then that rain would turn into snow, and if I got that upset that I cried hard…" His voice trails off. "Let's just say that a blizzard only happened once. And that was when Yahweh first confronted me about things."

"Jesus… That's scary. But what about when you get angry?"

"What do you mean?"

"Well you say it rains when you're sad, and that it snows when you cry. What happens when you get angry?"

"We don't know." I say. "There's never been a moment like that. When you've got angry and your weather powers have reflected that anger. But Yahweh only knows what would happen."

"I can only think of a storm or something." Aidan says. "Like, thunder and lightning could symbolise my anger?"

"Maybe. But I have a feeling that that's too close to your sad weather. There has to be a distinction."

"Maybe it's like, blood rain or something creepy like that?" Ben jokes.

"Could be." I say with a laugh. "Turns out you're terrifying when you get angry, Aidan."

He smirks. "Well, there's nothing scarier than the one guy who's always gentle with everyone when he gets mad. It's unexpected, which makes it all the worse." A smile crosses his features, and it sends a shiver down my spine. I realise that in caring about him, I don't want to be there when Aidan gets angry. Let alone to be the one who makes him angry.

We finish our card game, and I switch off the lights, getting into bed. *Tomorrow,* I think, *tomorrow we'll know where that barrier is. We'll go onwards to the Vatican and finally this matter can be resolved.*

# CHAPTER XI

When I wake up on Tuesday morning, I look over at Noah, dead to the world. His peaceful form makes me almost regret tapping him on the face to wake him when I see what time it is. Ben's flight is at four, so we need to set off for the Vatican nice and early.

"What time is it?" Noah asks with a yawn.

"Just after nine."

"Why'd you wake me then?"

"We're going to the Vatican today. We need to find the barrier now so we can go there tomorrow and pass through."

"Oh yeah…" His eyes shoot open wide. "Shit, it's tomorrow. When we're going to Purgatory."

"The penny drops!" I say loudly, and I go over to Ben. "C'mon, Sleeping Beauty, get your arse up."

"Aidan it's too early…" he protests, so I decide to leave him for a bit. In the meantime, Noah and I get dressed and we head downstairs for breakfast.

I help myself to a cheese and bacon croissant and some buttered bread rolls, while Noah takes some fruit from a bowl and a pain au chocolat. As we eat, I ask him how we intend on resting in Purgatory.

"We'll be able to pack up and sleep pretty much anywhere. There are alcoves in the rock that we can stay in."

"The rock?"

"Yeah. Purgatory is like a mountain, with rest stops along the way. It's designed so that everyone who passes through has to see each and every Sin, it's methodical. Nobody has ever bypassed a Sin, or if they have then that Sin has hunted them down."

I shudder. "Well I for one don't particularly want Lust chasing me for most of the way…"

"Funny you should say that, she's the first Sin. Don't worry though, we'll get her out of the way quickly."

"Okay…" I finish my food hastily, before downing my glass of water and briefly heading upstairs to check on Ben, with a small amount of food in a bag for him. I open the door and he's rushing around.

"Dude, what's up?"

He jumps. "Thank fuck it's you! I was scared you'd left me here for a minute!"

"We were just downstairs getting breakfast. You can

**130**

eat this on the train." I hand him the bag.

"No way am I risking eating it on the train, I'll end up spilling it on someone." He starts eating as I grab my day bag, and is just wolfing down the last crumbs of a slice of buttered toast when we see Noah outside the hotel.

"Ready, boss." I say, and we head to the underground.

After a somewhat better train ride, where Noah and I clasp a hand rail together, and Ben makes a beeline for a seat given up by a girl who gets off at the first stop, we get off and walk the short distance to the gates of the Vatican City. The man checking passports shoots me a strange look when I hand mine over, as if he knows me from somewhere, but he just mutters a quick 'move along' to me when he gives me it back. I thank him, and he does another double-take.

As soon as we pass through into the City, we see the huge spectacle of St Peter's Basilica, and Noah points to the very top of it. "Look. The pinnacle of the spire."

I look, and I can just make out what looks like a faint heat haze, but I see it shimmering with a multi-coloured glow.

"What're you looking at?" Ben asks.

"The top of the basilica, I think I can see the barrier through to Purgatory."

"I can't see anything."

"I think only we can see it, Aidan." Noah says. "It's meant to be undetectable to anyone but the angels. Sorry, Ben."

He waves a hand in dismissal, and we begin walking. Apart from the street vendors trying to swindle me into buying a selfie stick, and Ben stopping to get a photo with a nun, we're quite quick to get there. And to my surprise, not to mention Ben's irritation at having gone to the trouble of seeking one out for a photo, the gift shop is run by nuns.

"Good afternoon. Would we be able to go up to the top, please?" I ask the nun behind the counter.

She smiles kindly, a lock of blonde hair escaping from her habit and falling down across her face. "Of course you can. It'll be €10 though, I'm afraid, so it's rather dear…"

"That's okay. Do we just pay the nun over there?" I gesture to a set of steps leading further up, and a rather stern-looking nun standing near it.

"That's her. Enjoy your day, boys. And may God bless you."

She gives me another kind smile, and as I turn away and walk towards the other nun Noah whispers to me, "I doubt He's gonna be blessing us any time soon."

"No chance." I take out €15 to pay the three of us up to the spire and pass it to the nun, who gives me a small smile. We climb the steps and getting out onto the balcony we look out over the gorgeous landscape. The city walls are easily visible from the height we're at, but it's when I turn around that I get the biggest surprise.

Higher up, flush against the wall of the building, is a glowing portal. The ring around it shines with an iridescent light, and it's beautiful to behold.

"Noah, is there any way that Ben can see this?" I ask, my voice soft.

"Maybe. I'll try." He places his fingertips at Ben's temples, and says to him, "Now look at the spire."

Ben turns around, and jumps back, breaking Noah's concentration. "What's that?"

Noah replaces his fingers at Ben's temples. "It's the portal Aidan and I have to pass through. Nice, isn't it?"

"It's gorgeous. What's that inside it?"

We all look inside the portal, and I take a step closer. I can see a limestone mountain, and a huge staircase winding around it, dipping into and out of the rock. "That looks like Purgatory itself. The mountain that we've got to climb."

"It's huge. You sure you'll be okay? I could come

with you--"

"No." Noah interrupts him. "It's far too dangerous. We don't know if you'll be able to survive the jump into the immortal realm, nor do we know what it would do to you if you did survive. And I don't want to take that risk."

Ben seems somewhat disheartened. "Oh. Okay."

We descend to the bottom and, after seeing some more sights around the city, we board the train back to the hotel so that Ben can get his things.

The three of us ride in the taxi to the airport, and after Ben gets through security, we stand outside the gate. He foregoes the formalities and hugs Noah, thanking him for paying for the flight.

"It's no trouble. Think of it as repayment for me being such an arse to you that first day."

"You sir, are far too nice." He then embraces me, and whispers in my ear, "Take Yahweh down for me, dude."

"That's the plan." I smile. "I'll see you when I get back in a few days."

"See you."

We watch him as he boards the plane, and Noah casts me a worried glance. "When you get back?"

"I told you that I'd be returning to Orvale."

"Yeah, but don't you mean *we*?"

"Eh? You never said--"

"I know I didn't. But if you'd let me, I'd love to stay here with you, Aidan. We were such great friends up there, and it'd be such a shame to lose that again. Besides, the Lady has plenty of other angels who can do my job better than I can."

"Don't start again with this. You are brilliant, okay? You can only do the best you can do. And in case you haven't noticed, Asherah hasn't exactly been in a hurry to find a new angel of Peace."

He sighs. "Fine, I'll drop it. But still, I want to stay with you after this ends."

"Alright. But you'll have to pull your weight."

"Done." We start walking back through the airport to the taxi waiting for us, to go back there and spend a last night in the hotel.

We reach the hotel at half past four, and we're sitting around in our room when I ask Noah, "So what did Yahweh do to you?"

"What do you mean?"

"I remembered you comforting me after he first reprimanded me, but you were so upset about something. He'd spoken to you after dealing with me, and you said that He'd lost his rag with you since I'd been cast out. So what happened?"

A pained expression crosses his face. "Well, um…"

"Oh, you don't have to talk about it if you don't want to, I didn't want to upset you…" I say in apology.

"No, it's fine, really." He composes himself and looks at me. "Well, He'd been angry with me for being so close to you, and because we were such good friends, it irked Him for some reason. I don't know why.

"Yahweh had taken me aside beforehand and had told me that I wasn't doing well to associate with you, He said that He'd seen that you'd doubt His power. He told me…" Noah sniffs, and I can see his eyes shining. "He told me that I'd have to confront you about your…*deviance* was the word He used."

"Deviance? Meaning what, exactly?"

"I don't know."

I do. But I can't let Noah know. "Anyway, He said that to you. What happened after that?"

"Well the next thing that happened was that you raised your suspicions about Him. That was the first time He'd got angry with you, when we went out with Tom. Actually, I think we came here to see the basilica."

"That explains why the man outside the Vatican looked at me as if he knew me. Go on."

"So Yahweh had spoken to me about it and He'd advised me to avoid you. But I couldn't. You were so…nice about all of it and you were such a great friend to me, and I couldn't break what we had. So I kept hanging out with you. And then you doubted Him, and that's when we had the blizzard.

"But it all went wrong when you were cast out. He…" A tear slides down Noah's face. "He told me that you were a bad person. That you'd been blinded to the light, and when I defended you…"

Noah breaks out into full-on crying now, and it starts to rain outside. I gently take his hand.

"What did he say?"

*"He called me a faggot."*

The words are barely out of Noah's mouth before I grab him and hug him tightly. "Noah, you and I know the truth about Him. Nobody can take that away from us. And we're going to stop Him. We're going to make sure that nothing like this happens again, okay?"

Noah hugs me back, crying into my chest. The rain gets worse outside, and I contemplate what Yahweh said. *Why would he call Noah that? Unless…*

I pull Noah back, and my cyan eyes meet his blue ones. In a spontaneous movement, I press my lips to his.

# CHAPTER XII

When Aidan kisses me, I'm shocked at the revelation that he's that way inclined. But when I think about it, it's not that surprising. I'm more surprised that he likes me like that.

But to his credit, the guy's a good kisser.

When he pulls away gently, I wipe my eyes. "Thanks. I needed that." I smile, and he looks confused.

"Wait, you... You *are* that way?"

"Yep. You are as well?"

"Yeah." He gives a small laugh. "Guess I was just avoiding it."

"You? *I* was avoiding it... I wanted to kiss you right at the start when I came here! You're so cool, Aidan! Who wouldn't want you?"

He bursts out laughing. "Tell that to the guys at my school. Half of them would hate me for my sexuality, the others might be respectful, but..."

"But nothing. Ben and Cynthia would still love you for you, and if the others would react that badly to one little aspect of you, then they're like shadow friends. Staying with you in the sun but leaving you in the dark."

"Guess so." He looks out of the window, and I notice that the rain has stopped.

"Your powers." I say.

"What?"

"The rain. You were so sad when I told you what Yahweh did, and it chucked it down. Now we're fine, and the rain stopped. In fact," I reach down into the bag at Aidan's feet, and flip it upside down. A deep red rose falls into my outstretched hand. "The happiness you emanated has effects as well."

Aidan blushes, and I give him the rose before smiling to myself as I change into a different shirt for dinner. Aidan gets up and puts on a white long sleeved t-shirt with a swirling red design around the left shoulder and sleeve. When I've sprayed some deodorant on myself, Aidan puts the rose in a glass filled with water.

"It's pretty, is the rose." he points out.

"Well, it's you. It's the joy that you feel, put into physical form." I take my wallet from the bedside table, grabbing the room key and leading Aidan down to the lift by the hand.

We go down to the hotel dining room for dinner, sharing soft chewy breadsticks and each drinking a glass of Coke before our main courses arrive. Aidan orders a pizza with goat's cheese and various meats on it, and I ask for a pasta dish of farfalle with pesto and chicken.

As we eat, Aidan asks me, "So when did you know? That you liked me?"

"I think it was back in Heaven, when Phoebe asked me about you. You remember I told you I said we just clicked? I think I knew then that I felt more than just a click with you."

A smile crosses Aidan's lips. "That's sweet."

"What about you? Cause you obviously had your memory wiped, so when did you realise again that you liked guys?"

"Well I had a feeling at first, when Ben found me on the beach, that I liked him. But over time, that feeling just became a general liking rather than a romantic sort of thing. And when I saw you come down from Heaven, I just thought 'Do you want a side of *corruption* with your hot guardian angel?'"

The dirty expression he pulls makes me laugh, and he adds with a smirk, "You can guard me any day."

This sets me off even more, and I desperately try to calm down as the waiter shoots us a glare.

"*Scusa*." Aidan says, and I presume he apologised for us. I take another forkful of my food, and it's delicious. The Italians sure know how to make good pesto; the nutty, smooth flavour melds well with the chicken and the slightly sweet pasta.

Aidan seems to be enjoying his pizza, and he offers me a slice. "Only if you'll try some of my pasta." I tell him.

"Fine then." He smiles cheekily, and we swap our food over. I take a bite of the pizza, and the cheeses are sharp with the salty prosciutto and pepperoni, then the thick slices of salami on the top… I can see Aidan enjoying the pasta as well, for he asks me, "I'm really sorry but do you mind if…?" He gestures to the pasta, and I know.

"Yes, you can finish that off. Do you mind if I finish this?"

"Of course not, and thanks." He digs into the pasta, and I can't help but smile. He's so comfortable around me, and he knows that I'll never change my opinion of him as being so sweet and kind.

We finish our meals, Aidan thanks the waiter and asks about the WiFi as I head up to our room, letting myself in and sitting down on the bed, head in my hands.

"What am I going to do?" I ask myself. "If I tell him, then he'll hate me. But if I don't, then there's the chance that Yahweh will tell him when we get there, and then there'll be nowhere to run…"

I'm scared. Because I've kept something from him since the first night I spent here. As he enters the room using his own key, I flinch.

"What's up?"

"Nothing." I say quickly. Too quickly. Aidan comes and sits next to me.

"You seem tense. Seriously, what's wrong?"

I sigh, and decide there's no point hiding. "I have to tell you something. Since the day that I came here, I've been sending you visions." I confess.

"What?" Aidan looks confused.

"I sent you the memory of Yahweh attacking you when you fainted in class. I actually made you faint so you'd see it. That night I sent you the vision of Asherah and Yahweh. And the fact that your nightmares stopped when we shared a bed is no accident. I used my aura to repress the remnants of the memory retrieval. All you remembered was a stormy night, and I stopped that memory from disturbing your sleep.

"On Saturday night when you dreamt about me and about the Fall, I caused that dream. I showed you your memory, in the hopes that it'd unlock some of your other repressed memories. I've been instrumental in this entire flashback thing, and I knew that you'd

**143**

have a flash when we came here. The same with the Pantheon.

"Asherah knew exactly where you'd have flashes, and she told me to take you there and guide you through the memories. And for keeping this from you until now... Please forgive me."

Aidan is silent for several moments, before saying, "There's nothing to forgive, Noah. It's good that you showed me those memories, they helped me to recover everything now. If you didn't do that, then we might not be where we are now. I might not have believed you in the first place, I could have sent you packing.

"So you're overthinking things." he says kindly. "It's okay. I'm not angry with you."

I hug him tightly, and he hugs me back, gently running his fingers through my hair. "Thank you. For not getting mad with me."

"Who would get angry with you? You're so careful about things, you take every possible precaution to avoid a bad reaction. Why would I get mad?"

"Yahweh did."

"Yeah, but He got mad with me. And I'm pretty sure He's tearing up Heaven as we speak, so we'd better get up there soon. Now I need to speak to Cynthia, and I'll check the train times as well.

Do you mind if we get the earliest one?"

"Course not. The earlier the better to be honest." I say, lying back on the bed as Aidan goes into the en suite where the connection is strongest. *Thank Asherah for that!* I think in relief.

After he comes back in, Aidan tells me that the earliest train is at seven, meaning that we'd have to get up at half-six to check out and get to the underground. Deciding to eat in the Vatican, we each shower, pack up all but the essentials, and put our suitcases and day bags at the door before retiring to bed.

I wake up in the morning before Aidan's alarm, and I sit on the window ledge looking out over the city. The sun is still a way off rising, but the streetlights are bright enough for me to see things by. An Audi pulls up outside the hotel, the driver looking frustrated with his early wake-up call. A girl in a parka and boots wanders across the road, phone to her ear and breath coming out in rapid puffs of steam. And I catch a few bars of a song coming from the iPod in Aidan's bag.

I take it out and hold it to my ear to listen, turning down the volume so it doesn't wake him.

*Oh lights go down, in the moment we're lost and found, and I just want to be by your side, if these wings could fly... Oh damn these walls, in the moment we're ten feet tall, and how you told me after it all, we'd remember tonight, for the rest of our lives…*

The song makes me think of Aidan. Part of bravery is having the strength to not only stand up to those who oppress you, but also being able to be honest with those closest to you. It took bravery for him to kiss me earlier, and he comforted me in the way that came easiest to him, by showing that he cared.

I pause the song, and I wonder if Asherah would condone our relationship. Yahweh laid out rules against it, but changing values have shown that it's okay to be like us, to have that kind of relationship. So maybe She would, but He obviously wouldn't?

And if goodness and badness are absolute, then the Bible would qualify heterosexual love as good but homosexual love as bad. But love itself is intrinsically good (it is good for the sake of being good) and innately good (it cannot be anything but good). So love can't be bad, because it is always good, but a certain type of love is bad? The teachings in scripture are contradictory, but one thing that is constant is that Yahweh laid them down. So at one point the goodness in Him outweighed the badness, maybe; He could declare that love in itself is good, but then He also declared that certain types of love are bad.

I hear another sound that I recognise as Aidan's alarm. He turns over to see me sitting on the edge of the window. "Hey. What's up?"

"Nothing."

"Oh, okay." He gets up, stretches and sprays himself with deodorant before putting on his clothes. Dressed in a white long-sleeved top with black sleeves, a pair of dark black jeans, and his bright Converse, which he's dubbed his 'sunset Cons', he takes his bag and we head out the door.

We get down to the lobby and Aidan turns to me. "I've got to go and check out, you start walking and I'll catch up, okay? I don't want us to miss this train cause I spend too much time rabbiting on to the receptionist."

"Okay. See you in a minute." I take my suitcase and walk it down to the train station, which takes about ten minutes. When I pass through the ticket barriers, I hear loud footsteps behind me. Turning around, I see that Aidan is running towards me with his suitcase.

"Sorry I took so long; she wouldn't let me leave. The lass said I spoke beautiful Italian and tried to flirt with me."

"If I didn't know you better I'd be tempted to go back there and tell her to keep her hands to herself."

Aidan smirks, passing through the ticket barrier and we run to get a seat on the train. Surprisingly, it's not that crowded. We take a pair of seats at the front of one carriage, and as the train sets off with a jolt Aidan takes my hand.

I look across to him smiling brightly. "I can feel how nervous you are. Relax, Noah. Everything will be alright."

"You say that, but what if we've come so far to fall at the last hurdle? What if Asherah turns on us and She and Yahweh destroy us on the spot?" I ask desperately.

"She won't. I know She won't. She's the kind, loving counterpart to His angry malice. They balance each other, and let's face it, She sent you on this mission in the first place. Why would She reprimand you for doing what She asked you to do?"

"I know… I'm overthinking."

"You do that a lot." he points out. "No offence."

"None taken. But I need to work on it, I know I do."

"And there's no rush. We have time to get there. Asherah told you to get me as soon as you could, yeah?"

"Yeah. You're right." I clear my mind, and try to focus on my breathing. *Inhale, exhale… Inhale, exhale…*

Before I know it, we're stopping at the Vatican. We're getting off the train. And Aidan's got his hand in mine, leading me to the basilica. We greet the nun who let us up to the spire yesterday, and I can't help

**148**

but think she's suspicious when we pull our suitcases up the steps. But I don't let it get to me.

And now as I stand on the roof of the basilica, looking into the glowing iridescent portal, I attempt to use my aura powers to calm myself. But they don't work. I feel Aidan take my hands in his.

He closes his eyes, and whispers something in a language I don't understand. *"Sana animam hanc a fluctuationem iusto… Sana animam hanc a fluctuationem iusto…"*

"Aidan, what are you saying?"

*"Sana animam hanc a fluctuationem iusto…"* He stops, opens his eyes, and asks me, "Feel better?"

"I…" Surprisingly, I do. But…I was so doubtful of what we were about to do, so how could it have…?

"What did you do?"

"It's an incantation to calm you down. Now quickly, let's--"

Aidan braces my hand in an iron grip, and climbs up to the portal, jumping through it with his suitcase in one hand. He pulls me with him, and I let out a shout as we fall into the darkness.

In transitioning through the portal, I look around and see beautiful swirls of colour in the darkness. But the colours are dark, and when I look at them I just see the pain of the souls who've tried to come up through Purgatory.

I cast them out of my mind, and concentrate on what is in front of us. I see the huge mountain before us, and the staircase that we'll follow up it. My vision is directed to the ground, and we're spat out of the portal, heading down fast. I brace myself for the impact.

But it never comes. Mere inches above the ground, we're suspended as if levitating before our feet are on the earth. It's good to be back on solid ground.

# CHAPTER XIII

When we land on the ground in Purgatory, the first thing I notice is the look of the landscape.

It's surprisingly well cultivated, with a large amount of grass and other plants. The air is clean, and at the base of the mountain I can see the stone steps leading into a crevice in the rock face. I walk up to the mountain, and touch the stone. It feels like limestone, and there's no rainfall here either, so the stone wouldn't erode.

"It's hard to think that it's so difficult to climb. I mean, the mountain is easy to climb, being made of limestone, and the path is even there for us to follow." I note.

"But it's the inhabitants that make it so difficult. And it's not just the Sins. There are other things here besides them. Check your bag."

"Why?" I open my bag hesitantly, and there's nothing unusual.

I then flinch at a stabbing pain between my shoulders.

"What's wrong?"

"Nothing, I just felt something on my back."

"Hang on, let me check. I have a hunch…" I feel Noah slowly lift up my top, and his fingers graze the area at the very top of my shoulders.

"*Yes!*" he yells, and a huge smile comes over his face.

"What?"

"You've got the Mark!"

*The Mark?* "What do you mean?"

"It's a mark to denote you as an angel. It's shaped like a pair of wings, it appears on the shoulder blades of the person, and that person is an official angel. There's a tiny 'V' connecting the wings, showing that you're a Virtuous One… Oh Lucifer, I never thought this would happen, it's *great!*"

"Okay, so…" I take my top down, "what does this mean, then? Apart from the fact that I'm definitely an angel?"

"It means you've got your wings. Any and every power that you had before is now given back to you, and they're amplified here. So your weather powers will be stronger, and maybe they'll even become different in terms of manifestation. Meaning that maybe your joy power will be different to roses sprout-

**152**

ing from the earth."

"Or my sorrow not necessarily a rainstorm."

"Exactly. Your spells will be much stronger as well, seeing as you're able to tap into your angel aura rather than just your human aura."

"Hmm…" I wonder if my spells are only beneficial, or if they can be used for more…destructive purposes.

"We should get going. Oh, I almost forgot…" Noah opens his own bag. "I knew it was in here!" He takes out a dagger from his bag, which he fixes to his belt loops, and he tosses me a thick indigo tome. "That's been gathering dust since you left. I've been keeping it until I knew you'd be able to use it again."

"Thanks."

"The dagger will allow me to store any negative energy in the blade, so I can release it whenever I need to. You'll be able to cast spells whenever you want."

"Sounds great. At least we have more of a defence." We shoulder our bags, and open the book, finding the spell I want. I close my eyes, and sweep my hand across the suitcases. "*Evanescere ab oculis, protegam a nocentibus… evanescere ab oculis, protegam a nocentibus…*" The cases melt away into the air.

"Where did they go?"

"I vanished them. And even if He tries, Yahweh won't be able to find them; I cast a protection spell on them as well."

"Cool."

We finally set off up the mountain, and as we enter the cave, I take a flick through the book. There are incantations of all kinds, some meant to be sung rather than spoken, and one catches my eye in particular.

"Noah, do you know anything about this spell?" I show him the book, but before he can reply, we come to a large clearing.

"Brace yourself, here she comes."

"She?"

"Lust." Noah's face takes on a cold, unforgiving look. He draws his dagger and it glows.

I hear a shrill cackle, and a light comes down out of nowhere, growing brighter and brighter, until it then dissipates to reveal the form of a woman.

Her long bleached blonde hair falls down to her waist, and her skin is tanned a shade of bronze. She would be rather pretty, but her abnormally large breasts and backside detract from the modest looks. Her makeup is well done, but there's too much of it. She looks artificial rather than pure.

"Welcome! I've been simply dying to meet both of you!" She rushes forwards with surprising speed, clasping my hands in hers. "Aidan, the famous fallen angel! You defied Yahweh, and you're the reason He's so insecure... You've taken down Heaven! You're the kind of man I like, a rebel." She bats her eyelashes at me, and I feel a twinge of guilt for being so defiant in the first place.

Lust then grabs Noah by the hand. "And you, Noah. You've got a little secret, haven't you? You look for love that can't be true... You want this hunk right here, don't you?"

Noah chokes. "No! I don't want him like that... I love him, sure, but I don't... No, you're wrong!"

"Oh, but I'm not. I have seen your heart, and I know how it speaks. It says to me that you want what you simply. Can't. Have." She emphasises each word with a step closer to Noah, getting up in his face. "He doesn't want you. He could never want you, who would want someone who's so weak?"

"You're lying!" Noah shouts, looking to me in desperation. "Tell her, please!"

"Lust--" I begin, but she cuts me off.

"No, Aidan, you deserve better than him. You deserve me." She grabs my face and plants a kiss on my lips. I taste overly sweet tones of honey and sugar, and the taste makes me cough. I pull away from her and spit onto the ground.

"What are you doing?" I snarl.

Lust's face contorts into a look of shock. "What do you mean?"

"I mean you. Trying to seduce me. You're nothing but a temptress, and do you know the one thing Noah can give me that you can't?"

"And what's that, then?" Lust says, angry.

"*Love.*"

At the mention of the word, Lust covers her ears and screams. "NO!"

"Yes. He can provide me with pure, unadulterated love. Love that is patient, kind and protecting. Love, as opposed to the disgusting urges that you give."

In an instant, Lust's nails extend into long claws; at the same time, her lips become puffy and unsightly. She runs at me, but I dodge her attack.

I hold my hand out, palm open, and the spell book levitates in front of me and opens to a page. I read the incantation, and its effects on Lust are immediate.

"*Love is patient.*" Her mascara runs down her face, giving her an 'Alice Cooper' look. "*Love is kind.*" Her lips become chapped and crack. "*It always trusts, always hopes, always perseveres.*" Her nails break and fall to the floor. "*Love never fails.*"

Lust gives a piercing shriek, and begins to glow with a harsh, white light. Her breasts and backside appear to shrink to their natural size, her face returns to a rather beautiful fair, freckled complexion, and her

**156**

hair turns red. But her eyes are glassy and lifeless. She falls to the floor, and a breeze blows through the room, turning her to dust.

A fter we leave Lust's chamber, we keep climbing. When we emerge onto the mountainside again, both of us keep to the inside of the steps, and I take Noah's hand behind me.

Glancing down, I see a red glow far below us, past the base of the mountain. "Noah?"

"Yeah?"

"Is that...the Inferno?" I gesture down to the glow.

"Yes. It's the barrier between us and the fires below. And if you look really closely..."

I squint to make out what I see. I faintly see my own reflection in the barrier.

"It shows you how far you've come." I see that both of us have auras now, and our auras are tinted a rosy pink, denoting that we've overcome Lust. There's also a tiny 'L' on my dominant arm.

"So who's next?" I ask.

"Gluttony. And he shouldn't be too difficult."

"Okay." We continue our ascent, and after the path spirals around to the north face of the mountain we come to another entrance.

"Here we go." Aidan walks in, and I follow, coming into a chamber full of food.

Crates of provisions are stacked high against every wall, and each is marked. From fresh fruits and vegetables to meats and even desserts, whole meals are preserved in the boxes. I cautiously approach one at random, and open the catch on it. Apples spill out onto the floor, and I hear a booming voice.

"MINE!"

I jump back at the proximity, and a large being comes into view, sweeping his hands to send the apples back into their box using some kind of telekinesis.

The being turns to us, and I get a proper view.

He's huge, with a large grotesque stomach and a small face that is contorted in rage.

"How dare you touch my food?! You think you have any right to come here and to take what is not yours? This is mine! My food, to eat myself!"

"Gluttony, I presume?" Noah asks.

"Yes. And you?"

"I'm Noah, and this is Aidan."

His entire demeanour changes, and he becomes a squat, chubby young man of our age. "Oh! You're those two! Welcome, welcome! Please forgive me for my uncouth introduction, I can lose control when it comes to my food..." he says guiltily. "Both of you, please, feel free to help yourselves to anything you like!"

His change in attitude unnerves me, and I'm on edge. Noah seems to be as well, as he whispers to me, "Don't touch anything. He could get angry and flip out again if we do."

"But if we don't, then he could get offended at us refusing his offer." I reply, looking cautiously around. "And we *only take what we need*." I stress. "This is the chamber of Gluttony, remember."

"Got it."

I open my bag slightly, and siphon off some apples. Noah discretely snags a bottle of water and a quiche from an open box, and I ask Gluttony about a honey-like liquid in the corner, which has been decanted into several large flasks.

"Oh, that's Ambros! It's a gorgeous thing, like a honey water. It's so sweet and delicious, it'd be a shame to not let you take a flask on your way!"

"That's very kind of you, Gluttony. Thank you."

"Oh, it's no trouble, my dear lad."

I turn around to Noah. "Got everything?"

"Yep!" He shows me his bag, which doesn't appear to have changed in size.

But this seems to anger Gluttony.

"You… You didn't take anything? After I was so kind to you?" he asks, his voice rising.

"No, we did, we did take things, I swear!"

"Ah, so you're being gluttons, is that it? You're taking more than you need?!" he roars, growing in size and opening every box simultaneously with his telekinesis, so that we're overwhelmed by the sheer amount of food.

Apples, pies and gallons of Ambros flood the chamber, and the entrance is gone so that we're trapped against the rising tide. Gluttony utters a harsh laugh in triumph, but is then engulfed by his own excess, and I hear a faint shout as the food cascades down upon us.

A bright flash of light comes from behind Noah, and he grabs my wrist and lifts me up. We're hovering above the waves of food, and I turn to see that a huge pair of wings have sprouted from Noah's shoulders. We fly out of the chamber, and the food follows us, spilling out and falling down onto the barrier below.

Noah lands, and I brush myself off before he collapses onto the ground, gasping for breath.

"Remind me...to never...do that again..." he says, breathing heavily.

"What, am I that heavy?" I say, smirking.

He laughs, and says, "It just takes it out of me, flying again when I haven't flown since I was last in Heaven. And I've never flown with a passenger anyway, let alone one guy and two bags full of food.

"But hey, that's one more Sin down."

A thought then hits me.

"Oh! Hang on." I look down at my left arm, and see a 'G' a small space away from the 'L'.

"We've conquered Gluttony." Noah says. "But why the space between the 'G' and the 'L'?"

"I don't know."

We decide to set up camp after we overcome the next Sin, and make our way up the path, which now goes deeper inside the mountain, to a cave that is lit by torches. I see something gleam in the darkness.

"*Lux*." I say, and the room is enveloped in light, revealing that we're in a vault of some kind, with caskets of treasure and riches all around us.

"Wow…" I resist the urge to run over and open a chest, as that might alert Greed. But I hear a creaking, and I see that Noah has already picked up a chalice from a red casket.

"Noah, don't!"

A roar sounds from a large chest in the middle of the room, and a hunched figure leaps out of it.

"YOU! You tried to steal my treasure!"

"No, it wasn't his fault! He was examining your chalice, Greed!" I try and explain, but he picks up a handful of coins and hurls them at me.

The metal burns my skin on contact, and I hiss at the sharp pain, brushing off the coins.

He roars again. "You will both PAY for your crimes!" Greed points at us, and the coins fly straight for Noah.

He screams as the metal touches him, and I brush away the coins; angry red burn marks are all over his arms.

Greed takes a monetary note from a small dish, throwing it at us. It flies like a discus, narrowly missing me. He throws several more, and one clips Noah on the cheek, cutting his face.

"HA!" Greed then opens a chest full of gems, and hurls a diamond my way. I duck to avoid it, and it acts like a cluster bomb, exploding into more diamonds, which each explode once.

Brushing away the debris, I decide to give Greed a taste of his own medicine. Grabbing a large emerald, I toss it at Greed, and it blows up a large chunk of the white-hot coins. He snarls, before letting off a wave of the coins.

"Noah, throw whatever you can!" I shout, and the silver-haired boy chucks an entire dish of rubies and amethysts at the wave. Nearly every coin is destroyed in the blasts, and this only enrages Greed more.

But I can see that he is getting weaker. As his stock of treasure depletes, his physical form deteriorates.

Smashing up bricks of notes, I see him drop to his

knees.

"Please… Please, no more, I'll let you pass!" he says, begging me.

Noah shakes his head. I pick up a chest of gems using a levitation spell, and cast it aside into a mountain of coins and notes.

The entire thing explodes, and the rest of Greed's economy is in tatters. He falls to the ground, emaciated, and as his body crumbles into tiny coins, a small 'A' appears on our arms before the 'L'.

"What's the 'A' for?" Noah asks.

"*Avaritia*. It means greed, and we get our word *avarice* from it." I say, not knowing how I know. Must be the glossolalia. "But that's three Sins. And it looks like it's spelling out a word or something." I examine the letters.

"A, L, G…" Noah reads. "Does that sound like a word in another language?"

I shake my head. "Anyway, we'd better stop and rest. You said there were rest stops along the way?"

"Yep. And since we've defeated three Sins, then I guess we should just rest here."

I clear away any dregs of treasure, and cast a protective enchantment. Noah gets out a quiche that we recovered from Gluttony, and we eat by the light of my first spell before settling down to sleep under sheets that Noah takes out of his bag.

**163**

When we wake up, we get going quickly. Noah clears away the rest of the things into his bag, and yet again the bag doesn't appear to change in size or capacity. "What have you got in there?"

"Hmm…" He peers inside. "Makeshift bedding and food."

"And how can you fit all that into a little rucksack?"

"Easily." He unzips the front pocket and shows me the bag; it appears to be a lot more spacious on the inside. "I've got the bedding in the front, and the food in the back." He opens the second pocket, and I can see all of the food we gathered.

"What food have we got?"

"The rest of the quiche, bottles of water, the Ambros that Gluttony gave us, apples, loaves of bread, cheese, some different meats, and a few chocolate bars."

"You sneaky bugger, how did you get all that while I was talking to him?"

He gives me a wink. "I have my ways." Noah smiles, before looking up the mountain again. "Anyway, next up we've got Wrath. And he shouldn't be too difficult either. I think with Gluttony it was the element of surprise."

"But with Wrath, we know he'll try and attack us straight away because he's perpetually angry, so we

**164**

just have to be on guard." I say.

"Yep."

We carry on up the steps, and we come round the outside of the mountain to another clearing.

"Is this it?"

"Yeah. No boundaries." Noah says grimly.

A red flash alerts us, and a drop of blood appears on the ground. Several more droplets fall, merging into one large puddle which grows and becomes a vortex, out of which comes Wrath.

He's large and muscular, with small black eyes and a stress mark on his forehead. But when he speaks, his voice is surprisingly calm.

"So you're the two travellers who gave Lust so much trouble, eh?" he asks of us in a deep baritone.

"Yes." Noah says.

"Hm. Well it's a shame. I liked that girl. But I could never keep calm enough. I would always just LOSE it."

His voice flares on the one word, and I flinch slightly.

"But you... You can keep it under control. Especially you, Noah."

Wrath looks at him, and Noah wilts under his gaze. "What do you mean?"

"You're the angel of Comfort. You have to keep your cool, otherwise others won't. Your powers help regulate emotion. You too, Aidan. Your weather control centres around your emotions, and if you get too sad or, Yahweh forbid, angry, then it could be disastrous."

"Wait, wait... Wrath, do you know what would happen if I got angry?" I ask.

He nods.

"Can you tell us?" I follow up quickly, but Wrath just smirks.

"All in good time, lad. But what I can see... Heh, you'll need that anger. You'll really need to harness it if you want to take out the big guy." Wrath lays a heavy hand on my shoulder. "I could help you with that. I could teach you how to just turn it on and hit Yahweh with everything you have."

I have to stop and think for a moment. To be able to attack Yahweh at full strength, it would be tempting... To have that ability, it'd certainly be useful.

But this is Wrath we're talking about, Wrath who can't keep it under control to even speak to a fellow Sin. If he taught me how to use any anger that I have, I'd probably lose control like him. And I can't risk that. Not with being the angel of Bravery. There comes a point where bravery becomes rashness, and I can't let that anger make me reckless.

I look at Wrath. "So, kid? What'll it be?" He

offers me his hand to shake, and I take a breath, for I know what's coming.

"I'm afraid I'll have to decline. I can't risk being overwhelmed by anger, not with being the angel I am."

"The Form of the Brave, you mean."

"Yes. So I'm sorry, but--"

"Don't worry about it, kid. It's okay." he says calmly. "That's all I really have to say to you, so if you want you can be on your way."

"*What?!*" Noah bursts out. "Do you mean... You won't even fight us?"

"Nope. I'm trying to keep my anger under WRAPS!" He jumps at the strength of his own voice, and we flinch as well. "Sorry. Still working on it."

I smile, and offer my hand to him. "Thank you, Wrath."

He grasps it firmly. "Take care, now. And between you and me..." he leans close to my ear and whispers, "give Yahweh what He deserves."

"You got it, big guy." I let go of his hand, and he gives Noah a handshake before we exit the room, looking at each other in bewilderment.

"I wasn't expecting that..." Noah says simply, and we ascend the steps into the mountain, away from Wrath. An 'I' appears on our arms, making 'AL GI'.

"An 'I' instead of a 'W'?" Noah wonders.

"*Ira*. Latin for anger or wrath. And since *avaritia* is Latin for greed, then I suppose that the Latin names of the Sins make a word." I say.

We look up the mountain, and just as we start climbing, I swear that I notice a figure standing up at the summit, looking down at us.

# CHAPTER XIV

I see Aidan glance up at the peak of the mountain, and a look of surprise crosses his face.

"What's wrong?"

He shakes his head. "Nothing. Let's keep going."

"Did you see something?"

He nods. "A figure at the top of the mountain. I didn't get much, but they looked down at me and then turned away."

"So you just saw a silhouette?"

"Mm-hm."

"It can't be Asherah then; She radiates light. She's got a glowing aura about Her."

"Yahweh, maybe?"

"No. He wouldn't dare enter Purgatory. But I can't think of who else could be in here with us, besides the Sins." We continue to climb, and as we're halfway up a set of steps that branches over a chasm in the mountain, I make the mistake of looking down.

I see an endless abyss, and my vision blurs as if the blood pressure has dropped. I clutch my head, and I feel Aidan's arms wrap around me, steadying me.

"Whoa there, bud. Don't go dying on me now. We've come too far to lose it." he tells me, smiling.

I dig my nails into my palm to bring myself back. There are tiny crescent marks in my hand, but they're fading quickly. "Yep. Next up is Envy."

"Okay." We enter the mountain yet again, and an eerie green glow entices us into a bare open room. A thin man stands before us, sneering.

"I knew you'd come. You're both intelligent, smart enough to get past the others. Lust gave you some trouble, but you gave as good as you got." He chuckles, and walks towards us. "They wish they could have the job of picking off the last stragglers. Pride and I are pretty similar, you know. We get right inside the heads of anyone who comes this far. Cause they don't even know they envy anyone. But I expose that. I set free the deepest thoughts, the little nags that make you *green*." On the last word, Envy grabs my face.

"You wish you could be the angel who's got more Virtues. You wish you had some little quality that puts you above him." He jerks his head at Aidan. "You wish you could be kinder, stronger, better. *You want it*." He drawls out the sentence, and I pull away from him.

"That's not true!" I deny. "I accept that Aidan has better qualities than me, and that he's better than me in some respects. There's no denying that. But at the same time, we've all got things at which we're better than someone else. Even us angels are subject to that. Otherwise we wouldn't embody anything, we'd all be the same. And what's the point in that?"

"Yeah, sure. That's what they all say. But you desire that power, you envy it."

"No I don't. Even if I'm not the angel who has more virtues, then I'm gonna be happy for the one who is. That's the way it goes. And as the angel of Comfort, I can't go round upsetting others with envious thoughts. It doesn't fit with me."

Envy snarls, and turns on Aidan. "You then. What do you desire?" He grabs Aidan by the hair, pulling him up. Aidan's face twists in pain, and I have an instinct to stop Envy. But this is all part of the trial.

"What do you want? What is your one envied characteristic?"

"I don't want anything!" Aidan snaps, trying to resist.

"Oh, but you do! You want to be better, successful, you envy that success that others have!"

Aidan flinches. "Okay! I do envy it! I want to be successful. But don't we all? And if we're not

**171**

successful to the extent we want, then we'll make do, we'll get by. That's what we all do. There are plenty of people out there who have huge ambitions, and some might not reach those goals. They just need to look elsewhere to find their calling."

Envy retracts his hand, and retreats into the cave. "You...you admit it, yet you accept your envy?"

"Yes. I do. And I know that I'll try my damnedest to be successful. If I don't hit that mark that I want, then at least I can tell myself that I did my best." Aidan takes a step towards Envy, who goes further back.

"That's not how it works! You need to envy things! You need to *need* that success!" He's getting agitated, and I swear I can see a haze around him.

"But you don't. Success isn't everything. If I just have what I have now, my friends and my loved ones, then I'm happy. And that's not envy, as I already have it. You can't envy what you have."

"No! You're wrong!" Envy's eyes shoot open, and he glows a bright green. "I am jealousy, I AM ENVY!"

"Nobody's disputing you." I intervene. "This isn't about you."

"It is! I will make it about me!" He's clutching at straws now.

"See, now you're envying us." I tell him, and what happens next is a blur.

**172**

Envy snarls and lunges at me. Aidan clocks him with the spell book, and Envy bursts into a deep green fog.

After the dust settles, the Sin is nowhere to be seen, and I notice an 'I' etch itself into our arms.

"*Invidia*. Envy." Aidan translates. The word now reads 'ALIGI'.

"Does it resemble anything?"

"I have a hunch." Aidan replies. "Who's next?"

"Sloth. But I don't know what he'll entail." I say. We leave Envy's chamber, continuing up the path up the mountain.

"We'll rest up after this, then we can be prepared for Pride." I tell Aidan when we reach another cave. I let Aidan in first, then bring up the rear.

We ascend a steep stone face, coming to a large room full of fabrics and linen. I touch one of the sheets, and it feels soft, like silk. I see two mannequins over in a corner, and they wear identical sets of Greek-looking clothing.

"Why would Sloth go to the effort of making clothes?" I wonder, touching the belt of the uniform.

"Because I have too much time on my hands."

The voice makes me turn, and I see an elderly man at a spindle. He continues, "I got tired of being…tired, so I decided to take up spinning. I create garments now. And it just so happens that those suits

**173**

are for you two."

"Why would you do this for us? You're meant to stop us."

"No, I'm meant to challenge you. Wrath challenged you by offering you the ability to harness your anger. So did Envy, by extracting your thoughts and confronting you about them. I will now offer you help. These suits are perfectly self-sufficient. They will stop Yahweh like that." He snaps his fingers. "You don't have to do anything."

"That's impossible." Aidan says. "Yahweh is omnipotent, so He could shred these suits just by thinking. He could also stop the suits from damaging him if He so desires. You can't make a suit that is irresistible, as Yahweh is equally irresistible. His power is infinite, and so to match it would be absurd."

"You're correct there. But these... These have Celestial fabric woven into them. They can't be destroyed."

"Then Yahweh is not Yahweh."

"I beg your pardon?" Sloth looks puzzled.

"For Yahweh to be Yahweh, He must be omnipotent. And if He can't destroy these suits, then clearly He isn't all powerful, because there's something He can't destroy. But if He can destroy them, and as a result is omnipotent, then these suits aren't self-sufficient. We've reached a paradox." Aidan reasons.

**174**

A look of understanding crosses Sloth's face. "You're right. Good Lucifer...it's so obvious!" He knocks over the mannequins, destroying the suits in frustration.

He composes himself, and begins to weave.

"What are you doing?"

"Creating better suits for you."

"You don't have to. Just a simple outfit would be fine."

"Heh! Simple... Nothing here is simple, lad." In a flash, Sloth spirits extra cloths to his side and weaves them into the suits. A spiral of fabric and thread entangles itself in the garment, straightening out into a lining to go up the sides of the suit. In mere moments, I can see the suit coming together. A belt encircles the waist, and the off-the-shoulder outfit looks like a Greek chiton or toga; comfortable enough whilst still not restricting movement and being sturdy.

"Here. Try this on." he orders, brandishing the chiton at me. I get into the outfit, and it rests on my left shoulder, with a belt and clasp at the waist, trailing down over a thermal shirt and pair of pants. Two greaves and sandals allow for protection of my legs, and my arms are bare.

"How is it?"

"It's good. It should let us move perfectly well. Thank you, Sloth."

He smiles toothily. "It's no trouble, my boy. Thank you both for pointing out my mistake. And here's yours." He gives Aidan his outfit, and when we're suited up, I ask about our arms.

"How are we going to protect ourselves up here?"

"Pick out what you want from that pile over there." He gestures to a mound of gold battle ornaments. "I'll get on with my spinning."

I'm in shock. The fact that there have been several Sins who've let us go without a fight unnerves me. An 'A' appears on our arms, standing for *acedia*, or sloth, so Aidan says.

"ALIGIA. I've got it." He tells me.

"What?"

"Saligia was a Latin word meaning the collection of the Seven Deadly Sins. No wonder it's on our arms. It shows we've conquered them."

"Not yet we haven't. Pride is left." I say, sliding a gold guard onto my right shoulder.

"True." Aidan grabs two gold arm rings, sliding them up his right arm, and he lays a guard on his right wrist, laying a three-loop armlet on his left arm. He fastens a clasp on an identical anklet for his left leg, before straightening up. "Okay, I'm ready."

The golden armour shines modestly, accentuating the plainness of the fabric of the chiton. We turn and

**176**

look at Sloth. "Thank you again."

"Don't mention it." he says, returning to his spinning.

We leave the cave, looking in shock at each other.

"Guess there's only Pride left." Aidan says.

"Yep. And there he is."

We come to a stone slab, on top of which stands Pride. He is muscular, dressed in only a pair of shorts which expose his chest. His face is handsome, but something about him sets the hairs on the back of my neck standing straight up. It's unnerving.

"Well then. Sloth helped you?" he asks with disgust.

"Yep." Aidan says, showing him the armlet. It almost winks at Pride in the low light, and a scowl comes over Pride's face.

"Don't get cocky with me. We all know Sloth's given up. He doesn't want to be a Sin any more. Wrath as well. They're cowards, both of them. Envy never really tried to stop you, Lust underestimated you, and Gluttony and Greed were lenient. It's only me who's capable of stopping you."

"And you're calling me cocky." Aidan scowls right back at Pride.

"Well I'm Pride, ain't I? It's my job to be better than everyone else, I'm the last Sin people have to face before they reach the top. I've got to be the best, otherwise why would I be right up here?" he says, swaggering towards us.

"Then are you going to keep blowing smoke?"

"You what?!" He's snapped now. "I'll make you regret that, kid!"

Pride summons a ball of energy, projecting beams of black at us. Aidan holds out his hand, spell book in the other hand, and creates a light shield to protect us.

The beams are absorbed, and the shield turns from a pale green to a cyan colour.

"What the hell? You can't do that, you little twat!" he swears.

Aidan doesn't reply, and Pride continues to blast us, with Aidan's shield absorbing every blow. The shield quickly turns from cyan to yellow, then to red, and finally to black with the force of the energy.

Aidan brings his hand in, then throws it out at Pride, and the shield creates a shockwave that knocks Pride down. His eyes glow a fierce gold, and Pride raises his voice.

"You dare to attack me? You, a mere spellcaster, when I am a Sin?!" he roars, and Aidan's face is stony and unchanging.

He approaches Pride. "Evidently you're not as powerful as you thought. Some Sin you are." His voice is soft, but not arrogant. He's stating a fact.

**178**

A horrified expression comes over Pride's face, and golden light emanates from Pride's eyes and mouth, causing his body to be lost in the strength of the blast.

When everything settles, an 'S' has appeared on our arms, making the word 'Saligia'.

# CHAPTER XV

"Alright. So that's the last one, we're home free!" Noah shouts happily, and he runs up the steps, with me following.

"We still have to get into Heaven. If there's a gatekeeper, then we might have to fight them." I say, the thought only just occurring to me.

"Yeah, but we'll be alright though." The joy on Noah's face makes me feel warm, as if the power of his smile is simply enough to ease me.

I smile back at him, and we carry on up the mountain. The path does another revolution around the mountain, and then stops, letting us walk up the rock the rest of the way.

But as soon as we're back round to the south face of the mountain, and the steps stop, I see a figure in the distance.

"Aidan, is that who you saw looking down at you before?"

I have to squint to make out the person, and they do seem familiar. "I think so. I'll ask them."

We approach the person, and they topple over when we get close.

"Shit!" I run to their side, and I see that it's a woman. She wears a long, flowing dress that looks as if it's been torn at the sleeves and hem, and her skin is pale. She looks emaciated, and I clasp her hand.

"What happened to you?"

"Ugh…you…"

"Are you okay?"

"You two…you need to carry on. Don't worry about me."

"What do you mean, how do you know us?"

"I've heard the word up the mountain. You've been taking down Sin after Sin. Just look at your arms, you're on a mission." She traces the mark on my left arm, and her fingers are thin and spindly.

"Well, we have, and we are, but that doesn't mean we can't help you. Here." Noah reaches into his pack and takes out a bottle of water, handing it to the woman, who sits up, holding her head. She downs a few mouthfuls, and takes a deep breath.

"That's gracious of you." The woman pours some water onto her hand, and wipes her face of the dirt. "I feel better. Thank you, both of you."

"It's no trouble." Noah says, sitting down on a rock

to speak to her. "Are you hungry?"

Her stomach growls before she can answer, and he takes out the rest of our quiche to give to her.

"Oh, thank you!" Her voice is rough and crackly, but after the woman eats, she washes it down with some water and her voice smoothens out.

"Ahh, that's better." It has a certain melody to it, and it's high and pleasing to the ear. "I feel like myself again." She gives us a warm smile.

"That's great." I sit down next to Noah, and she joins us on an adjacent stone.

"So who are you both?" she asks us.

"I'm Aidan, and this is Noah. We're hoping to go to Heaven."

"I know that." She laughs. "But why are you particularly hoping to go there? You don't look...dead." she says bluntly. "In fact, you look familiar. I can't place you..."

Her eyes then shoot open wide. "Oh, Asherah... I do know you. You're the pair of angels who want to destroy Yahweh."

"How do you know that?" Noah asks sharply.

"Wrath told me. As soon as he let you pass by, he informed me. I've watched you up the mountain, and I must say, *you* were quite harsh when you fought Lust." She nods to me, and I shrug.

"She made allegations. I defended myself."

**183**

"I suppose so. Even so, you're both good looking lads. I'm surprised you're not using this time together to continue your relationship."

"As you said, we're on a mission. A relationship can wait until after this."

"Smart boy." She nods.

"Anyway..." I say, "We've told you who we are; who are you?"

"Well..." She sweeps her long black hair away from her face, brushing it over her shoulder. I can see that she wears a pendant over her chest, and a black rose corsage on her wrist. There is an 'A' etched into the pendant; it's a teardrop shape, and the bead is held in place by a leaf-shaped clasp. The bead itself shimmers in the darkness, glowing with a pale light.

"Who gave you that?" Noah asks.

"The necklace? My ex-husband." She smirks. "He was so sweet to begin with, then when I made one little mistake he left me."

"That's awful. I'm sorry."

"It's okay. I've learnt to survive on my own. And Adam was never going to stay with me, he ran off back to *her* after he'd finished with me." A disgusted expression crosses the woman's face, and the name she mentioned makes me wonder.

"Adam...?"

"Yep."

**184**

I look down at the ground, trying to make the connection, but Noah gets there first.

He gasps. "*Eve*."

She nods solemnly. "Adam left me for the other bitch after I got us kicked out of Heaven."

"Bitch? Who do you mean?"

"Lilith. She was Adam's first wife. But she refused to be subservient to him, so he ditched her and made Yahweh craft him a new wife, me. I was made to obey Adam's orders. Then when it went downhill, Adam only went crawling back to her. The serpent tricked me into eating the fruit of the Tree of Knowledge of Good and Evil, but looking back on it, it was the best mistake I've ever made.

"It opened my eyes to the horrors of the world, and how cruel Yahweh is. Asherah pitied me, and She saw Adam leave me. She offered me to re-enter Heaven under a different name, to try and fool Yahweh, but I refused. I'd rather live on my own than trust Him again. Either of them, Adam or Yahweh."

"I'm so sorry. Is there anything we can do?"

"There is one thing." She takes my hand and squeezes it, looking into my eyes. "You can destroy Yahweh for what He did. He ripped my fucking life apart. And why would He even create the Tree if He knew I'd be tempted by the serpent? He knew that I wouldn't be strong enough to resist, yet He does nothing to stop me. If I didn't know any better, I'd think he wanted us to sin.

"So if you would be so kind, Aidan, take him down."

"It would be our pleasure, Eve." Noah says, and I nod.

"Here." She takes off her necklace and gives it to Noah. "It'll help you."

"What? I couldn't take it. And how would it help me?"

"Adam gave it to me, and Asherah gave it to him because She knew I'd need it. I think She knew there'd be trouble ahead. Since I've been here, that necklace has served to protect me. And the corsage was a gift from Asherah when I came here." She takes it off and fastens it around my left wrist. "I don't know exactly how, but I know that they will aid you. Otherwise Asherah wouldn't give me them."

Noah puts the necklace on, and it rests against his chiton. "Thank you."

"It's no trouble at all. There's something else I need to tell you, about the Sins.

"You see, they weren't always Sins. They were just regular souls, who came through here. And Yahweh chose them at random to be the embodiment of each Sin; he twisted their psyches beyond repair. Wrath and Sloth are the only ones who resisted, and they tried to regain control of themselves. Wrath was unusually kind, yes?"

"He did seem a bit...off, compared to our perception of him." Noah points out.

"Exactly. He fought Yahweh's control, and Sloth deviating from his job of being a lazy Sin couldn't have ground Yahweh's gears more. But Wrath and I...we're not that dissimilar. We'd both devote our whole lives to achieve the end that is best. We'd happily see Yahweh destroyed, and that's why we helped you.

"But if you do take out Yahweh, we'll all change back to who we were before. And the other Sins are too in love with their twisted selves that they don't want that to happen. Wrath, Sloth and I are more than willing to make that sacrifice."

"Wow. Well, um...thank you, Eve."

She hugs us both. "You saving us all will be repayment enough. We'll be spared the agony of Yahweh's insatiable hunger for control and power."

I'm about to say something, but I'm interrupted by a voice.

*"THERE THEY ARE!"*

It's a shrill, screechy voice, and I turn on my heel to see that the Sins have returned. Lust points a threatening finger at us, and her artificial looks are even more grotesque than before. Her makeup has run, her breasts are still over-inflated, and her hair is far too brightly bleached. Gluttony is waddling towards us, his stomach making him trip up every so often. Envy is glowing, his sneering face becoming more prominent with a lavender tinge on his skin. Greed's skin is marked by burn marks from his own coins, and I can just make out Pride walking alongside Lust, his muscles bulging and his face contorted in rage.

Lust sprints towards us, attempting to claw at my face, but I throw out an energy field to repel her. Eve takes a pearl out of her dress pocket and hurls it at Gluttony, who explodes in a shower of half-digested food. Greed tosses a ruby at Pride, and he then blasts it towards Noah.

Noah kicks the ruby down the mountain, and I can just see it detonate below us. "We need to go."

Eve takes an entire pearl string from the same pocket, spilling the beads across the stone to subdue the Sins with a cluster of explosions, and pushes us towards the top of the mountain. "Go! Get to Heaven, change everything!" she shouts over the sound of the beads.

"What about you?" I ask desperately.

"They can't catch me! I have eyes all over this mountain!" Eve replies, and I hear a loud, guttural roar below us.

Wrath is bounding up the mountain, his muscles and physical strength sufficient to pull him up with surprising speed. And I can see Sloth with his spindle, ascending on a mountain of fabric. As he spins the thread, it creates sashes that entangle Lust, Pride, Greed and Envy. Wrath then destroys them by delivering a ground-shaking impact to their bodies.

They reach us, and Sloth smiles. "I see that those outfits came in handy."

"We haven't had much of a chance to test them yet." I say.

"Either way, you seem perfectly capable of handling yourself, lads. Go kick Yahweh's celestial arse." Wrath lays a hand on my shoulder, and I nod.

"I've given them my gifts. They've had all the help we can possibly give." Eve says, and Noah and I turn to head back up, saying a fond farewell to Sloth, Eve and Wrath.

We travel a bit further up the rest of the mountain, and the path flattens out. I can just see a light in the distance. It looks like some kind of gate.

"There it is! The entrance to Heaven!" Noah shouts, overjoyed.

We both set off into a run, and the gate comes into focus. It is in the shape of an enormous arch, with the golden sides of it creating some kind of portal, as I can see a cultivated mass of vegetation and flora on the other side. And I can just make out a silhouette standing in front of the gate.

She's a woman, wearing a flowing dress that is bunched up at the waist and held by a belt. She faces away from us, and so I can see that She has a large pair of white shining wings coming from Her shoulder blades, as Noah did when he rescued us from Gluttony's chamber.

On Her feet are bound a pair of sandals, and Her dress reaches down to the ground, ruffling at the hem and revealing that there are three layers to it; one purple layer sandwiched between two white layers. The woman turns around to face us, and Her eyes shine with a kind, innocent light. Her face is pretty, and Her hair is a shade of brown, quite like my own, stretching down Her back to Her belt. She carries a thin wand-like staff in Her hand, with two snakes coiled around it; a caduceus.

We approach Her, and She smiles, opening Her arms wide.

"You did it! You succeeded, oh, my dear sweet Noah..." She runs—or rather glides—towards us, embracing Noah.

"You're not unhappy that it took so long?" Noah asks uncertainly, and Asherah shakes Her head.

"I could never be unhappy with the effort you make

**190**

Sure, I've pushed you all in the past to embrace your abilities as angels, but that was only because I've wanted you to do your best." She lets go of Noah, and looks me over. "Aidan."

I sink to the ground in a bow. "My Lady." I'm expecting Her to be angry, but Asherah embraces me too, as I imagine a mother would, and I can't help but weep.

"I deserted you... I hurt you by invoking Yahweh's rage... I'm so sorry, Asherah..."

"Aidan, sweetheart, don't be sorry. You were only doing what you thought was right. You acted innocently, and it was wrong of Yahweh to lose control. He knows that, but is not willing to admit to it. He is encased in His insecurity, and we've all had to walk around on eggshells, out of fear of this god who calls Himself our Lord."

She looks at me, as Eve did, and kisses me on the cheek. "Don't ever feel that you must repent for being nothing more than yourself. You are the only thing you can be. You're kind, you're brave, and you're extremely patient. You embody not just your own Virtue, but those of several; Peace, Bravery and Comfort."

She then stops. "No. There is another, one more who embodies the Virtues. And that one," She turns to Noah, clasping both of our hands, "is you, Noah."

"What?" he blurts out, covering his mouth. "Me?"

"Yes. You embody the same as Aidan; Comfort, Bravery and Peace. Both of you have great courage in standing up for yourselves to not only your enemies, but also to your friends, and to each other. You're not afraid to fight for what you believe in, and your exchanges with Wrath and Sloth when climbing the mountain show your bravery as well, as you resisted the potentially easy way out. You weren't afraid of rising to the challenge.

"You've been extremely peaceful in dealing with the Sins, both choosing to debate with Lust, Envy and Pride rather than engaging in physical conflict. Gluttony and Greed were overcome by their dark hearts, and so fought you with great fury, against your preference.

"And your comforting souls have been shown through your dealings with each other in the mortal realm. Noah, you calmed Aidan's heart by dispelling his nightmares, and Aidan, you aided Noah by being a shoulder for him to lean on and an ear to listen to him. Yahweh would refuse to hear him out, and he never thought to ask me out of fear of being a burden to me. Isn't that right?"

Noah looks at the ground sheepishly. "Yes, my Lady."

**192**

Asherah smiles knowingly. "You both have to realise that people choose to associate with you for a reason. You both have hearts of extreme purity and characters of great strength. Therefore, your friends who care about you, Aidan, and the other angels, Noah, have just as much respect for you as you for them. They love you for who you are, rather than who you attempt to be in order to appease them."

Asherah waves Her caduceus above our heads, and the snakes which adorn it disentangle themselves and slither onto our arms. They lick our dominant arms with their forked tongues, and the word 'saligia' disappears before they resume their positions around Asherah's staff. "Proof of your entrance into Heaven. The Sins catch up with everyone, and should someone evade them, Eve has correspondence with them so that she can guard the gate. And even then, they must get past our guards. So one way or another, everyone must have the writing on their arm, in order to have it absolved." She explains.

"So Eve herself was the gatekeeper…" Noah says.

"I wanted to apologise for Yahweh's expulsion of her from Heaven, and gatekeeper was the only role she'd take." Asherah shrugs. "Speaking of Yahweh, we must end this feud once and for all. Wings out, my angels."

Noah and I instinctively spread out our arms, and I

feel my wings materialise from the Mark on my back. I take out my spell book, which glows softly with neutral white light, and Asherah's eyes widen in joy.

"You gave it to him!" She says to Noah. "This is brilliant! Aidan, you need to let your emotions reign over you when we face Yahweh. They will be your greatest asset."

"Okay." I channel my happiness at being here into the book, and it glows a bright yellow-orange with the positive emotion.

The three of us step forward to the Gate, and we pass through into Heaven.

# CHAPTER XVI

As soon as we get into Heaven, however, the scenery instantly changes.

Trees wither, the greenery turns a toxic purple, and all of the beauty drains from the landscape, as if sucked out of it by a vacuum.

Asherah stands horrified at what has become of the place. "What happened? I don't ever remember it being this bad... Unless..."

She screams in realisation, and Her hands fly to Her mouth. "No!"

"What's wrong? Why is Heaven like this?" I ask.

"Both of you, listen to me. This is a side effect of me stepping outside the barrier. I supply the Garden, which in turn brings vitality to the entire atmosphere of Heaven. We need to find the Garden."

"You don't mean...?"

She nods. "We must go to Eden."

Asherah's wings immediately retract into Her shoulders, as do our own. I flinch at the sharp pain of it, but Asherah begins to tremble.

"It's Him. He's doing this…"

"Who?"

"Yahweh. He's found us." Her voice cracks, and She draws Her caduceus. The snakes start to hiss, and out of nowhere the fog dissipates to reveal a figure standing before us.

His robes are of a shining white, His face terrible and furious. Yahweh grabs Aidan by the throat, shouting. "You were banished from this place! How dare you return!"

Aidan's choked breathing spurs me to take his spell book from is hand, open it to a page, and shout an incantation. "*Dimittere eum!*" Yahweh throws Aidan from His hand as if burned, and I hand the book back. Asherah then takes Her caduceus and stands in front of us, facing up to Yahweh.

"How dare you hurt them?" Her face is contorted with sorrow. "How could you bring yourself to harm your own creations?"

Yahweh shakes His head in disgust. "They sinned by breaking away from me. The first doubted me, and the second left voluntarily."

"All of us are your children!" I shout. "You chose

to banish Aidan, and it was that which sent me away
to find him. This was your doing."

Yahweh snaps His fingers, and a fleet of
centurions appears out of thin air, swarming us.
"Allow the gods to have a little chat!" He roars, and I
see Asherah pleading with Him as we're swept back
by the tide of bodies.

I draw on my Virtue of Comfort to attempt to calm
the centurions, but all it does is make them stop
moving. The entire fleet draw their weapons, and
Aidan casts his hand towards them. Two large swords
and shields appear, and we take up arms.

"We have to fight them, Noah."

I hesitantly take a sword, sliding the shield up my
left arm. I focus on deflecting the blows dealt by the
centurions, whereas Aidan knocks them to the ground.
I see that as soon as they are downed, the centurions
appear to melt into a pool of liquid, like blood, and
disappear. However upon Aidan touching the liquid,
something strange happens.

He becomes enveloped in a bright golden light,
and his physical appearance changes as well. His hair
grows slightly longer and changes to incorporate a
streak of silver, his body becomes more muscular, and
his wings return. In addition, the gold bands and

adornments turn a shade of bluish-green, and Aidan's eyes flash dangerously. His chiton has become a robe of white material, and I can also see that the word 'fortitudo' appears across his chest.

"The Form of the Brave." I realise.

Aidan opens his arms, and every centurion melts in a shockwave generated by his body. He then takes my hand gently, guiding it to the pool on the floor.

Instantly, a golden light consumes me, and I change as well.

My body fills out, as Aidan's did, and my attire changes into the robe that he wears. My wings return too, and the golden adornments I wear become a shining white, like platinum. My silver hair now falls down my back, held by a large clasp into a billowing ponytail, and a streak of brunette runs right through it.

The word 'solatium' marks itself on my chest, and Aidan translates it. "Comfort. It looks as if the blood of a centurion enables us to achieve the Form of our Virtues, or in our case the one Virtue that is greater than the others; my bravery and your kind, comforting nature." he explains, hugging me tightly.

I don't know how to feel, I'm overjoyed that we're able to take on Yahweh, but the fact that we had to dispose of a centurion to do that… It troubles me, as I could have ended the life of another being.

I dismiss this thought, as we must take on

Yahweh. We rush through the atmosphere of Heaven, which is still rather withered and broken.

Instead of the flourishing nature that used to adorn the place, the grass and greenery is shrivelled and poisoned, as if tainted. The usual green is replaced by the same dark purple shades we saw earlier, and although most of the fog is gone, there are still clouds of the poison gas around. Flowers are wilted, the formerly beautiful trees are black with corruption, and any fruit that grew on them is now dead.

I hear a shout, and turn to see that Asherah is facing off against Yahweh. He's summoning barrages of energy to try and hit Her, but She's just managing to fend off His attacks with Her caduceus. The snakes are swallowing each blast to protect Her, and blowing smoke with every exhale.

I look at my sword, and see that it has now become a sceptre. I thrust it at Yahweh, and send a pot-shot of pink energy His way. It hits Him on the shoulder, allowing Asherah to strike Him with Her caduceus. The snakes spit venom at Him, and His robe tears.

Yahweh's eyes flash with anger, and He grips Asherah by the throat. "You dare to oppose me? You, the subservient and inferior?"

"Leave Her alone!" I shout, running at Yahweh, and Aidan begins to chant a spell.

**199**

Yahweh tries to hit me in the stomach with an energy bolt, but Asherah throws her caduceus to intercept the blow. The staff breaks in two.

She falls onto Her knees, with a staff piece in each hand, and I can see tears streaming down Her face. The caduceus itself is snapped cleanly, but the snakes' bodies are lifeless.

"You're a monster!" She says bitterly, and Yahweh looks upon Her with contempt.

"Seeing as you continue to defend these sinful creatures, I have no choice." He leaves in a blaze of blue flames, and Asherah's eyes light up.

"NO!" She screams, and She is overcome by a fierce determination. Asherah warps us both to another place in Heaven, and what I see astounds me.

A huge meadow greets us on all sides, sprawling and green, with an enormous willow tree in the middle of it. I can see thousands of blooming flowers around us, roses and daffodils arranged in concentric circles around the tree. Several other trees are dotted further out, and I can see a stream of crystal clear water running past us. I cast my eyes back to the tree; the fruit on the tree are perfectly circular, and are a matte white colour, as if dipped in white chocolate. They hang low, just low enough for me to reach, but Asherah stops me.

"Don't eat one." she warns. "That's the Tree that

led to Adam and Eve being kicked out of here."

"The Tree of Knowledge?"

"Knowledge of Good and Evil. Yahweh didn't want another being to know everything in the world, especially not the secrets of good and evil. He didn't want it to be known that He failed in creating a perfect world."

"Because He didn't want to?"

"Because He couldn't. He's not powerful enough, nor is He good and benevolent enough, to create such a world." Asherah's voice hardens like stone, and I hear Aidan say something.

"I'm sorry?"

He looks at me, his eyes burning a bright blue. "I said that the spell is ready. When you give the word, I'll cast it."

"And what is that spell?" Asherah asks.

"Here." He opens the book and shows Her a page, but She gasps.

"You can't! That would destroy us too!"

"Not if I draw on the Form of the Good."

She nods in agreement, picking a fruit from another Tree a short distance away. "Listen carefully. This will let you access either the Form of the Good or the Form of the Evil. You must choose the Good, as it will be the only way to stop Him."

"I understand." He takes the fruit, which closely

resembles a golden apple, but Yahweh arrives then.

His voice almost shatters my eardrums with the depth and volume. "Both of you are vicious beings! You deserve death for your disobedience!"

"No! Please!" Asherah begs of him, but Yahweh literally throws Her aside. She immediately tries to come back to us using Her wings, but She meets a barrier. I hear Her pounding on what looks like an invisible wall.

Yahweh sneers. "Stupid girl. I am omnipotent, don't you remember?"

She attempts to shout, but no sound comes out.

"Heh. You're hopeless."

"You're wrong." Aidan says, discreetly pocketing the fruit.

Yahweh turns His face towards Aidan. "What?"

"You're not omnipotent."

"You dare to oppose me even now?"

"Yes, I do." Aidan's voice hardens. "And you're not omnipotent, because if you were, you wouldn't require six days to create the Universe, nor would you need a seventh day to rest. And since you're not subject to change, you can't change your mind or decide to take a day of rest. You're meant to be the ultimate efficient being, able to do anything possible in as little time as possible. If you'd merely put your mind to it, you'd create an entire perfect Universe in a mere split second.

"What's more, if you created a perfect Universe, and everything in your world is perfect, then there would be no evil. There would be nothing for the Tree of Good and Evil to signify; as there is no evil, so there is no good either. Everything is perfect, and we need evil to appreciate good, so both terms are obsolete.

"Your omniscience was your downfall, as you forbade Adam and Eve from eating from this tree, yet you knew that Eve would be tempted by the Serpent. If you created her perfect then she would have resisted temptation, and because she isn't perfect, then neither are you, as a perfect being can only create other perfect beings, meaning that you are imperfect for being unable to create her perfectly. She ate from the tree, yet you knew that this would happen but did nothing to stop her.

"You're a liar. You foretold that you were perfect and omnipotent and everything else, knowing full well that you weren't. Lucifer doubted your people's faith in you, but nobody had ever questioned your ability until I did, and you banished me for it because you were insecure about your shortcomings.

"You're no better than we are, you're subject to all of the things we humans are. But that's not necessarily a bad thing. Sin frees you from perfection, and just as

Eve did, we've seen what you've done to this world in damning its people and being unthinking about how your actions will affect your creations."

The depth of Aidan's words sinks in, and Yahweh's expression changes once again to one of rage.

He throws His hand out towards Aidan, and prepares to strike him down. "You have been a thorn in my side long enough, child! *Take THIS!*"

The next few seconds are blurred.

A huge ball of energy forms in Yahweh's hand, and He throws it straight at Aidan.

The barrier around Asherah comes down; She screams, and the sound makes both Aidan and I clamp our hands over our ears and fall to the floor in pain, as it's a sound that I never want to hear again, a cacophony that makes my hair stand on end with the instinctive feeling that something is horribly wrong.

And my adornments shine brightly as I dive over Aidan to take the energy blast meant to kill him.

# CHAPTER XVII

Is what's happening really...real?

I see Yahweh fire a huge blast of black energy at me, but I'm forced to the ground by Asherah's pained voice.

Noah then shields me from Yahweh's attack, taking the full brunt of it instead of me.

And now, as the dust clears, I open my eyes and see that Noah's body lies lifeless on the ground, turned to stone by the force of Yahweh's anger.

I can't comprehend what's happened, he can't be dead! Yahweh can't kill one of His own angels, can He?

I take the stone face of Noah in my hands, and my voice comes out rough and breaking. "Noah..." I take in all of the hollows and contours of his face, perfectly captured in the stone. "No... *NO!*"

I burst into tears, and hug the statue tightly, with a light sprinkling of snow beginning to fall. The light snow becomes a blizzard quickly, separating me and Noah from Asherah, and obscuring Yahweh.

I cry myself out, sobbing over Noah, and the glow from my spell book turns an icy blue to reflect my sorrow. I remember the times we shared together, both in Heaven and in Orvale...

*I* *first saw him standing on the sand, with silvery hair just falling to his shoulders, and framing his face in a side-swept fringe. His clothes were simple; a plain white top with grey jeans and white shoes, but I remember he had eyes of brightest blue, like the sky on a clear day. They shone like diamonds, reflecting every other light that passed through and showing it in all its beauty. In the same way did Noah's personality match this, as he would point out other people's good points and put positive spins on any negative, as he did with me.*

*His voice was smooth and soft, showing how peaceful he was; even when he was frustrated or upset, as he was when we were in Orvale, he had a high and melodious tenor voice, which was always pleasing to the ear. Come to think of it, he praised my singing when I brought him back to Orvale, yet he never sang with me. It's a great shame.*

*When we were in Rome, he seemed to relax slightly, as if he was truly home. We saw the Pantheon, and his concern over me when I had a vision was heart-warming. He seemed genuinely scared for my well-being, as if this wasn't his intention, to scare me. But if anything, it helped me to accept what I knew would come when we faced Yahweh.*

*Then his confession after Ben left…*

*That hit me by surprise. It was well-received, mind you, but it came out of nowhere even so. And I suppose that when we were together, and definitely when he left for Heaven, I felt so much love for him. I wanted to take back everything I said when he left, and then when he came back I just lost control and hugged him.*

*Every night I spent with him, I guess my feelings grew. Not just my romantic feelings, but also the feeling of general friendship. Like we were re-establishing what we had in Heaven before Yahweh cast me down. Or at least that's what it felt like.*

*But Yahweh… Why couldn't He just leave us alone?! Is it that much of a crime to love someone else? And for two angels to love each other, nonetheless? After what Asherah said about us both sharing three Virtues, it was as if he and I were…as clichéd as it sounds…made for each other.*

*And after what Lust said in Purgatory, berating Noah for loving me as if I disliked him for being nothing more than who he is, who we both are, it was awful. Granted, she was meant to challenge us, but it was as if she genuinely wanted me, and genuinely hated Noah for loving me. If you care that much about someone, even just as a friend, then one little aspect of their personality, like sexuality, shouldn't change your perception of or attitude towards them.*

*He was beautiful, he had an immensely pure and kind heart, and he embodied three Virtues that anyone would respect.*

*And I loved him... Well, I say 'loved'... I still do love him.*

*I love him.*


My wings flare up when I stand after what feels like an eternity.

My tears are still wet on the stone face of Noah, indicating that it was a much shorter time than I thought, and the book stops glowing.

I still feel sad, but I feel so much anger.

Towards myself, for not protecting him, even though he protected me.

Towards Asherah, for sending him to Orvale to fetch me, and dooming us to fall in love. But for that I can forgive Her.

And towards Yahweh, for casting me out in the first place.

The book glows black.

I turn and look at Yahweh. The blizzard has stopped, and something is raining from the sky. But I can't tell what it is.

Asherah catches my gaze, and Her eyes narrow as

She understands what's going through my head. She nods grimly, before raising her shield, which I recognise as being similar to Athena's aegis.

A burst of pale light emanates from the aegis, and the bracelet that Eve gave me resonates with it, glowing white in response. A circle appears under Yahweh's being. The first circle, or layer, immobilises Him, and in a flash another larger layer appears with runes around it. It glows a turquoise colour, and a third layer materialises with more runes. The three layers glow a bright black, and my book hovers in front of me, opening to the page I marked earlier.

I take a bite of the golden fruit, and the taste is so bitter that I spit it back out. But it has the intended effect; a white light creates four extra wings from my back, changing me into a seraph. The wings change colour, becoming iridescent and seeming to phase through every colour imaginable, and the word 'bonum' appears across my chest, denoting me as the Form of the Good.

And as the book's black glow intensifies, I finally realise what is raining from the sky as it drips down my face, thick and warm.

*Blood.*

*So this is what happens when I get angry...* I think, wondering why it didn't happen sooner.

Yahweh's face shows something I've never seen

before in Him; fear. He attempts to use His power on me, but something in my face stops Him. The book's pages glow white, urging me to read.

My voice comes out as a creeping drawl. *"Conversus rubrum in caelo est... convertimini ad virtutem adpropinquavit... decidet me lacrimis purpura caeli... solvere leges et lapideos!"*

Thunder roars overhead, and the blood falls thicker, drenching Yahweh and myself; Asherah is covered by a barrier that She conjures. The layers of the circle in which Yahweh is trapped start to spark and crackle with energy.

*"Adtendite ad horam animadverterent... Tempus labitur!"* I draw out the last word, and the energy generated by the barrier grows.

My voice rises, until I am screaming the incantation. *"Intra sanguinem de clavium! Cruentaque horrorem! Partum opus meum, nunc regnabit SANGUINE!"*

I let out a guttural scream at the end of the spell, and the barrier shatters as the sparks overwhelm Yahweh and He is vanished in a cataclysm of blood and black energy that disintegrates His very being.


The light dissipates, and what is left of Yahweh is blown away in a breeze that courses through

Heaven.

Asherah lowers the barrier around Herself, and waves Her hand over me. My four extra wings are gone, and I return to my normal angel form. I retain the silver streak in my hair, however, as well as my turquoise armour. I've also gained a scar across my cheek.

I breathe a sigh of relief, and look at Her. "Does that qualify as wrath?" I ask guiltily.

"No. He deserved all of that and more. Your spell cast Him down to the inferno, rather than outright destroying Him, and so He must suffer the same fate as you did. He is banished to your mortal realm, and likely has been hit with amnesia as you were, Aidan." She says.

I look over at where the statue of Noah was, but it is now gone.

"What happened to it, I know that we left it right here!"

Asherah smiles kindly, leading me over to a small glade. I see a crowd of angels, all of whom I recognise as the other Virtuous Ones. They all look in our direction, and as soon as they see me with my armour they swarm me in joyous chatter.

"It's so good to have you back!"

"Thank you so much for helping us!"

"Dude, you kicked his arse!"

**211**

"Nice anklet, Aidan…"

This sarcastic comment comes from Tom, whom I then give a fist bump. "Says you with your necklace…"

He smirks, and shows me the pendant. I recognise it as the one that Eve gave to Noah, and instantly do a double-take. "Where did you get that?"

"See for yourself." He steps back, as do all of the Virtuous Ones, to reveal the statue of Noah. Asherah glides past us and touches the statue with Her shield.

"*Vive.*"

The stone falls away from the body underneath; Noah's eyes open, and he takes a breath of life.

# CHAPTER XVIII

I fling my arms around him, tears streaming down my face.

"Oh my god..." I sob, falling onto my knees and letting Noah hug me.

He smiles down at me. "It's okay, Asherah revived me. Just as Yahweh has the ability to destroy, so does Asherah as his opposite have the ability to create. Or, in my case, bring back from the dead. And we're technically already dead since we're in Heaven. We can return, mind." he explains, but I can't process anything apart from the fact that he's there with me again.

I sniff and wipe the tears away from my face. "I thought I'd lost you."

"I'm your guardian. If anything, I'd be losing you, but I'll never let that happen." he says, and I stand up, turning round to face Asherah.

"You don't know how happy you've made me, my Lady."

She opens her arms, and hugs both of us. "I have to protect my Virtues. For you're not only my children, but you're also my dear friends. I love every one of you." She looks at us. "And you saved Heaven. That merits some form of reward."

Noah looks at me to go first.

"Well, if it's alright with you, my Lady, I only wish to return to the mortal realm." I say, before quickly adding, "Don't get me wrong, I love you guys, and you were my family before I was cast down, but my new friends in Orvale were there for me when I was at my lowest ebb. So I hope you understand--"

"Of course I understand, my dear boy. And it was never up for debate, where you would reside. I would only ever have left it up to you." Asherah says.

"Oh. Okay, um…" I give a nervous laugh. "Noah, could you…?"

He takes the hint and speaks. "I only wish to live with Aidan in Orvale. Him and me having each other's backs is all I'd want."

Asherah smiles broadly. "Look, I know you want to be together, but you're asking for things that are already there for you. I appreciated that you'd fallen for each other, and I guessed that you'd want to both live in the mortal realm. C'mon, ask for something I can grant you!" She laughs.

I pause for a few moments, but nothing comes.

Nothing that I already have, at least. And I don't want to be greedy and ask for something I don't need.

"With all due respect, my Lady, there isn't anything I would like. Save my reward for a rainy day." I sink to my knees in a bow.

"Hm. That's a very noble decision. I know I made a good choice when I selected you both to have three Virtues. And Noah, what is your wish?"

"That we can pass through the barrier to Heaven, and see you guys, whenever we choose. If that'd be possible." he says, bowing as I did.

Asherah's aegis glows softly, and our adornments glow in response. "Done. Your armour is your pass to Heaven. Simply wear your armour as you would in Heaven, and you will be able to pass through should you desire."

"Asherah?" I ask.

"Yes?"

I suddenly become sheepish. "Um... I know you said before about me being noble, so I feel like I shouldn't ask..."

"No, it's fine, Aidan. Go on."

"Well... If you'd be able to now that Yahweh is gone..." I take a deep breath. "Would you be able to let Eve back into Heaven? And return the Sins to their human forms?"

She smiles, and gestures to the heavenly gates. As

if on cue, a group of eight people passes through the gates.

An elderly man sits at a spindle, a pretty redheaded girl in a saffron gown is laughing with a modestly muscled young man whose eyes have a good-natured shine to them, another lad with well-toned muscles is conversing with a slender older man, and a teenage boy is tossing a coin up into the air while a second boy watches with a bag of sweets in his hand.

Another girl stands apart from them, wearing her torn dress and with her long black hair falling down her back.

"Eve!" I shout, and I run over to the group.

Their heads turn, and they all shout to us. "Aidan! Noah!"

Eve hugs me, and the man formerly known as Wrath smiles and nudges Sloth, who is spinning a pair of socks. "I told you they could do it."

"I never had a doubt." He nods to me, and I give a nod back.

Lust comes over to us. "I want to apologise for my behaviour when you were in Purgatory. It was horrible of me, and I'm sorry if I upset you, Noah." Her freckles are accentuated by her pale skin, and her red hair sways in the wind.

"It's no problem, Lust." Noah says, taking her hands gently.

"Oh, it's Lucy. Not Lust."

"Lucy. Okay. Have all of your names changed?"

Pride comes over to us. "Yep. I'm Paul, and Wrath is now Will. That's Sidney over at the spindle, and Greg is trying to barter with Georg for his sweets. Then Ed is the one who's skinny as a whip." he smirks.

Ed gives us a curt nod, and the twins Greg and Georg wave. Will gives me a friendly wink, and Sidney's too busy at the wheel to acknowledge us a second time.

"As soon as you defeated Yahweh, we all felt ourselves changing." Paul continues. "We all fell out of love with our evil hearts, and when we saw the light emanating from Heaven, we knew that we had to return. Eve was the first to notice, actually."

Eve shrugs. "Only because I was closest to the gates. And cause Will and Sidney stayed with me when we took you lot down at the pinnacle."

Ed looks down. "Yeah, sorry about that…"

The others mumble apologies, but Asherah silences them with a wave of Her hand. "You are all forgiven. It was Yahweh who put you under the curse of the Sins, and again it was He who cast you out, Eve. And because He is now vanquished, you are absolved of your Sin status, as well as your other misdemeanours so long as you pledge your service. If you

**217**

wish not to be involved, then I understand and you may return to the mortal realm with Aidan and Noah."

"I'll happily serve you, my Lady. If it will help to rebuild Heaven, then I will devote myself wholeheartedly to it." Eve says, curtseying to Asherah.

She taps Her aegis, and Eve's appearance changes. Her dress, once ripped and torn, becomes a floor-length gown with a sweetheart neckline and wraparound sleeves. Noah and I give back her bracelet and pendant, and white designs adorn the hem of the dress. Eve's hair becomes a long ponytail, similar to Noah's when he assumed the Form of the Comforting.

"Thank you, my Lady."

"I should thank you, Eve." She nods to Eve, who takes a place beside us. "Who's next, then?"

The former Sins instantly agree to helping to aid Heaven in its recovery from Yahweh's reign, and Noah and I go back to the other Virtues.

After several hours spent catching up in Eden, during which Phoebe remarks at how cute it is that Noah and I are seeing each other, Asherah and Her entourage, which consists of Eve as Her secretary of sorts, and Lucy, Paul et al. as Eve's team of advisors who will work closely with the Virtues to watch over the world and ensure that things will get better from here on out, come over to escort us back home.

So when it's time for us to leave and return to the mortal realm, I find myself saying goodbye to the others safe in the knowledge that tomorrow will be better, and that we have the power to make it so.

I hug Lucy and Eve, smirking when they tell me to 'look after that boyfriend of yours', and Paul surprises me by asking if we can meet up outside of Heaven at some point.

"Sure, if you want to."

"Cheers dude." He's about to shake my hand, but decides against it, instead outright hugging me. "I feel like I can be honest, and I hate how I acted towards you guys. I was so arrogant, and seeing as you're so modest and kind, maybe you could help me out a bit?"

"If you want." I repeat, smiling as Noah and I prepare to leave.

I wave to everyone, looking out over the serenity of Heaven. And as we open a portal and are about to travel back to Orvale, I swear that I can see a young man in Grecian clothes and winged sandals standing behind Asherah, wearing a quiver of arrows on his back and holding a beautifully well-kept bow. The man gives us a salute and a warm smile, and I hear a voice in my head, pleasing and melodious.

*Don't worry. Everything will be alright. We will rebuild what He has destroyed, and together Heaven will rise again from the ashes.*

"Thank you, Apollo." I whisper, and he smiles.

*Thank you, Aidan. You freed me, as well as the rest of us, from Yahweh.*

I then see several others come into focus behind Apollo; Demeter, Hera, Hestia, Aphrodite, Artemis and Athena stand beside him, before the goddesses merge into Asherah in a flash of light.

She nods in confirmation, and my vision turns black as we cross through the barrier.

I can hear the sound of waves gently lapping at sand, and the smell of salt water comes to me. I open my eyes and lift myself off the sand, looking around to see that the sun is just rising on a Sunday morning, and I'm on the beach behind my house.

Noah is a foot away from me, and I gently shake him awake. "Noah, wake up. We're back home, we're in Orvale."

He opens his eyes and smiles. "Hey. I know where we are, I woke up about five minutes ago. I wanted to just lie here and take everything in." he says calmly.

We both stand up and brush the sand off our clothes, but I notice that we're dressed in our regular clothes, devoid of our armour or robes.

"What happened to our...?"

"I don't know. I'll go and check inside." I say, heading up the steps and unlocking the door. A parcel is on the dining room table, and a note is placed on top of it.

Noah enters the room as I begin to read. "'I never got a chance to introduce myself properly, but this is my thanks. I hope you both find it satisfactory.

"'Apollo.' So he *was* standing behind Asherah in Heaven?"

"I saw him too. And the other goddesses." Noah says. He unwraps the parcel, revealing two small hinged boxes of polished maple wood. He hands me one box, taking the other and opening it up.

I open mine, and it contains a white winged emblem with a large diamond in the middle. Gold and red coloured enamel accents border the diamond, and it shines gloriously. I remove it from its cushion of crushed indigo velvet, and although it's fairly heavy, it appears as if it will fit into something.

I mention this to Noah, who shrugs. "Maybe. Let's go check where our armour is first."

I walk through into the living room, and nothing is out of the ordinary. I then hear a voice from upstairs.

"Aidan, you need to see this."

I head up and Noah opens my wardrobe. It's become larger, and Noah opens a panel at the back to reveal another compartment. Our armour, adornments and robes hang on mannequins, and there is a gouged-out indentation in the shoulder plate. I take the emblem and fit it into the slot; the armour glows brightly, and the emblem fuses with it, becoming a design moulded onto the plate.

"Try it on." Noah suggests, and I suit up, fitting the anklet around the leg of my jeans and the armlet around the sleeve of my top. A glow resonates from behind me, and Noah gasps.

"What?" I turn to look in the mirror, and I jump at what I see.

A pair of wings have sprouted from my back, and they gleam pure white apart from a few cyan feathers here and there. They add to the overall look, however, the blue and white.

"That must be what it does. When we wear it with the armour, it denotes that we've earned our wings." I conclude.

I place the armour back on the mannequin and shut the wardrobe before Noah hugs me tightly.

"Aidan, I have to thank you. You were willing to go through all of that shit with me here, then you went with me through Purgatory, you stood up to Lust for me… And you took Yahweh on… I love you so much."

I smile meekly. "I love you too." I cast a glance over to my nightstand, where the spell book is sitting.

I notice that it's changed since I had it in Purgatory. It's bigger overall, and a gold design adorns the front and back covers of the deep purple tome. Opening it to the front page, I see that more spells have been added, and that most of them are very tame, such as a soothing spell. The more aggressive spells are near the back of the book, and are marked with a Post-It note.

It reads: 'In case anything like this ever happens again. A.'

I can't determine whether the 'A' stands for Asherah or Apollo, or indeed both, but it seems as if Apollo has become his own entity in the destruction of Yahweh. Just as Noah was my own guardian, so is Apollo the guardian of both of us together. And the goddesses reside in Asherah, so that solves that. I assume that the six of them and Apollo are watching over Heaven as Noah and I are standing here.

"So what now?" Noah asks me, and I smile.

"Now, I get to live life normally. And love life with you."

Gabriel Williamson hails from Skipton in North Yorkshire, England. Besides authoring *As Heaven Does*, he is a talented actor and singer. This is his first novel.

## ACKNOWLEDGMENTS

There are only a few people to whom I would like to dedicate this book, more than anything because it was quite a solitary affair. I chipped away at it with little outside assistance, and so these acknowledgements will be few and far between. Not to say that these people are any less deserving of acknowledgement.

First, to Cade Jay Hathaway and the whole team at Cerulean Sky. None of this would have been possible without you.

Next, to my local theatre school back home in Skipton, for instilling in me that the show must go on, so to speak, and for never letting me give up. I love you guys.

To my dear friend Josh Ellis, for sticking with me throughout the process, and constantly asking me when he was going to be able to read my work. Today's the day, mate.

Finally, to my family, notably my mother and stepfather, for supporting me in all the decisions I make, and for always believing.

—GW

Printed in Poland
by Amazon Fulfillment
Poland Sp. z o.o., Wrocław